No Prince for Riding Hood

ANNA KATMORE

To Riley.
A very special character.
Without the whisper of your tale
I still wouldn't know who I am.

Whispering Pages

Book 1

Chapter 1

Every time someone opens a storybook and reads the four magical words *Once upon a time...*, my granny gets eaten a few hours later. Boy, it sucks!

Glad that this morning's staging of our play is over, I slip into Princess Cinderella's castle and close the heavy door. The loud thud echoing off the high ceiling makes me cringe, and I quickly place a finger in front of my lips. "Shhh!"

Yes, doors actually listen. I believe they even talk, but that might just be a rumor Alice brought home from

Wonderland.

I toe off my scruffy boots next to the coatrack. Their soles still bear half the forest after today's adventure, and I don't want to mess up this immaculate place. I slip off my yew bow and quiver from my shoulder. The twelve cedar arrows rattle inside as I hang both on a hook on the wall. One doesn't waltz fully armed into a tea party—or at least that's what they keep telling me. I push off my hood but leave the red cloak on.

Wide, marble stairs with golden handrails invite me to the other side of the great hall. An invitation I cannot refuse. I sprint up, taking two steps at a time, and turn left at a junction to a long corridor. My friends' laughter drifting out from the parlor farther down tells me which room to enter.

Four princesses are seated around a neat, white coffee table with morning tea in delicate china cups before them. Once again, they are all dressed in marvelous, colorful gowns. I wave in greeting and then steer toward Snow-White. The princess with hair as black as a raven feather hates her name and once said she'd much rather be called something cool like Rocking Thunder. Ever since that day, we keep calling her Snowy.

I slump down next to her on the noble sofa with its gold-embroidered, blue cushions. Her white skirt accidentally catches beneath me. As she tries to tug it free, I help her by quickly lifting one side of my bottom. Then I pull up my legs and wrap my arms around my knees with my cloak tugged close, mimicking a stark, red iceberg floating among the royals.

Cindy slides a cup of strawberry tea across the table in front of me. "Hey, Riley, what rained on your parade?" Her porcelain face splits into a grin as she leans forward, briefly blocking the beams of sunlight shining into the warm room through the five tall windows. "Did the Wolf bite you on the ass again?"

Right, maybe what I said about *Once upon a time* before wasn't entirely the truth. In some fairy tales, the girl actually knocks into a prince who kisses her, loves her, marries her, and gives her a giant closetful of gowns in his palace. At least, it's like that with Snow-White and Cindy. In Belle's story, too. Dang it, Aurora aka Rory doesn't even have to do a whole lot for *her* happily ever after. Toward the end of her tale, she just lies down for a short nap, and Prince Phillip takes care of the rest. All my friends get kissed and fall in love, over and over again. Not me.

"Man! Do you even know how lucky you girls are? I want me a prince, too!" I pick up the chipped cup on its saucer. "At least they don't bite."

Belle hides a snicker behind a cookie, and a light flush appears around her nose. Okay, so maybe her prince does, but I don't believe the Beauty minds.

"Well, well." With a curious gleam in her green eyes, Rory tosses her wavy, golden hair behind her shoulders. She sits up straighter to face me. "Didn't you always say that boys were good for nothing and you weren't interested? When did you change your tune?"

Yeah, when? Must have happened sometime after slipping on the wet forest floor in the dead of night because some weird child in a faraway land called The Reality couldn't wait until the morning to read their new storybook. Then a monstrous wolf almost ate me at dawn because he was still hungry after being forced to give back my gran. The new fang marks on my left butt cheek will shine for a week!

"The whole fairy tale thing is so unfair." I sniff the tea and pray I won't shoot to the ceiling like a giant. Things like that have occurred in this castle before, when the Caterpillar and the crazy Hatter were around for a visit. Ever since that crazy afternoon, I make sure to check the coatrack for a hat sized 10/6 or for a hundred pairs of tiny shoes in the corner before touching any darn food in this place!

"Out of us all, I got stuck with the short stick." After the first cautious sip of tea, I squeeze my eyes shut and wait a panicky second, but nothing happens. *Phew!* Relaxing, I drink some more. "I want my own happy ending. A *real* one! With a real prince who will kiss me and love me and take me to his castle." I stir the tea with a silver spoon and watch as the red-tinted water swirls around. "Not a guy who smells like a wet dog in the rain and prefers to crawl into my granny's bed instead of mine."

Not that I would ever want Jack in my bed. *Ew!* A spooky shiver travels down my spine at the image. Okay, he actually is some kind of gorgeous. At least on days when he doesn't grow a wolf skin and put me on his menu for dessert. But those days are rare. And even then, he isn't right for kissing or marrying. He simply lacks the manners for that. And, evidently, the crown.

"So you think you can only find romance with a prince?" Aurora smothers a yawn with her hand. She, too, had to act out her tale today, and is obviously still suffering from the aftermath of her sleep curse—even though the spell is broken. "What makes you believe they're any better with love stuff than other guys?"

"Well, that's obvious, isn't it?" I put my cup down, nail her with a meaningful stare, and then tick off my next points on my fingers. "*You* have a prince. Snowy has a prince. Cindy has a prince, and Belle has one, too." Fair enough, Belle's Prince Dominic might be a little hairy at times, but he is one of the blue-blooded thugs in Fairyland, after all.

Snow-White puts some honey into her tea and daintily licks the rest off the spoon. "And in your eyes, love comes with a royal title and a palace? I mean, there are thousands of tales in the world, and not all have a prince in them."

"Exactly what I'm trying to say!" I fold my arms over my chest. "Peter Pan is no prince, and Wendy is still single. Duh!"

"Hm. Your logic is unassailable." Cindy taps a finger against her bottom lip and cuts a look at the ceiling. "Alice never warmed up to the Hatter, either."

There we go! "And you all know Dorothy, who gets a Scarecrow, a Tin Man, and a Cowardly Lion? She keeps clicking her heels together to go back to Kansas. Every time." I make a stern face. "Hence…no prince, no romance."

"Wait a moment. What about Aladdin and Jassie?" Rory counters, making me snap my head to her. "Aladdin is a thief and, obviously, they can't keep their hands off each other."

"Naah. Jasmine's a princess," I point out. "In their tale, the roles were just switched."

"True." Snow-White scratches her chin. "Jassie always wore the pants, long before she even met Al."

"You might be onto something here," Belle supports me now, pointing a finger my way as she narrows her eyes. Then the Beauty gets up from her chair and paces back and forth in front of us. Her heels clack on the stone floor underneath the hoop of her marvelous purple dress. She can never sit still for long, especially not when she's pondering. "The list of royal love stories in this country is long. Even the red-haired fish girl—" She whirls around to us. "What's her name again?"

"Ariel," we all groan and cut her tired glances. For some stupid reason, she constantly forgets the mermaid's name.

"Ah, yes. So she gets Prince Eric, right? Ann-Marie marries the Frog Prince. And Rapunzel is a kidnapped princess herself."

"See?" I raise my eyebrows and gesture wildly with my arms. "Love only happens among royals. Nobody has ever read about a girl from the woods falling for a verminous pooch."

Rory lifts her nose, disgustedly pushing away her cake and wiping some crumbs off her pink dress. "Ugh, you think Jack has fleas?"

I shrug it off. "Sometimes, I see him scratching his ear with his hind leg when he's in wolf form, but that might be out of habit." He actually does it a lot when he's nervous. And he always gets like that before the ending of our story. I probably would, too, if the Huntsman was going to cut *my* belly open with a knife to free my latest lunch.

Ignoring our speculation about Jack's hygiene, Princess Cinderella leans across the coffee table and pats my hand. "So, not all fairy tales end with love. That's just life."

"Yeah, but if they don't, at least those characters get to do some cool stuff in their stories." I grab my ankles, my feet still flat on the couch. "Take Hansel and Gretel, for instance. No romance, but an entire house full of candy to crunch. What do I get? A small piece of cake and wine, and I'm not even allowed to eat it because the basket is for Granny."

Cindy tips her head to the side and presses her lips together. I don't know how to interpret her look. Five seconds later, she grabs a platter from the table, holds it out to me, and lifts one eyebrow in hope. "Macaron?"

I drop my forehead to my knees and groan.

*

"Don't hang your head, sweetie." Cindy hugs me tightly in the great hall after our tea. The other girls left an hour ago, so I had some time alone with my bestie to swoon over the hotties in the latest issue of *The Character Magazine* and read about the most recent escapades in Fairyland. Delivery weasels tend to get distracted in the woods and misplace parcels. I'm missing two months' worth of issues, so I have to rely on Cindy these days to provide my weekly celebrity fix. Her charming husband picks up the magazine for her from the *Magical Press* each Tuesday, right after it releases.

Another advantage of having a prince at hand. Just saying.

While I tie my boots, Cindy squats down in front of me and places her hand under my chin to make me look into her starlit eyes. "You know you didn't get the worst deal with your story."

That's easy for her to say. As soon as this heavy door closes behind me, she'll skip into the study, drag Prince Jason into the living room, and cuddle up to him in front of the home cinema.

The only thing I can cuddle up with is the old blanket on my couch. Or Jack Wolf, who recently ate my grandmother. I prefer the blanket.

But I give a quick nod anyway and smile courageously at my friend. As we both rise again, she holds out my bow and quiver.

"You're right." It's not the worst story in the forest, just one without romance. "I guess I could be a green witch and get squashed by a house at the end of my tale, right?" That would really screw up my day.

She laughs, but I see the shivers spreading over her bare arms at the mention of the Wicked Witch of the West. That woman is a grumpy old hag, and not only in her story.

"Come to the market with me tomorrow?" Cindy changes the subject as I turn and open the door.

"Sure," I call over my shoulder and wave goodbye as I leave Castle Grove, the home of most of my princess friends. "Meet me by the fountain!"

She didn't actually have to ask me to come. Strolling through the market of Grimmwich with my best friend on Mondays is as much a non-changeable tradition as the stories we each play out. Even though she's generally the only one who buys anything. But that's because I don't have a chamber filled with treasure to spend on excessive luxury. I don't own a castle, remember?

But it's okay. The forest provides whatever I need to survive: food, wood, and animal skin. The rough life in the wilderness has turned me into a formidable archer, and I'm excellent at fending for myself. Besides, Granny is a great tailor. Sometimes, she designs me new clothes. Simple garments made of linen or the leathers I bring her after skinning my prey.

This pretty, hooded cloak is one of the first things she ever made for me. Apparently, a fairy gave her the red satin many, many years ago, and it's supposed to always protect me from harm. I broke my wrist last summer…so much for the protection. Still, I don't ever take it off. Well, I do. To sleep. But that's it.

It's why they call me Red Riding Hood.

Unfortunately, shoes are something I do have to spend money on. I look down at my feet as I tramp through the Wood of 1000 Dawns. These boots are barely two years old, practically brand new. Certainly good enough to walk another decade in. To raise the money for this pair, I had to paint all the white roses in the Queen of Hearts' wondrous garden red. No shit. Not a very grateful job.

Behind a line of hazel bushes up ahead, I see the straw roof of my cozy little hut. A thin trail of smoke from the fire I made this morning still puffs from the chimney. A warm feeling floods me at the sight. There's hardly any interesting booty for thieves to steal in my house, so the square windows stay open all summer long. As I approach, a robin, usually nested under the roof, greets me from the window ledge with a happy chirp. I pluck a raspberry from the shrub winding up the pole of the porch as I walk up the steps and place it in front of my tiny friend with a smile. "Enjoy, sweetie."

No matter how much I sometimes wish for a different ever after for myself, I always take in a deep, happy breath when I cross the threshold of my cabin. Sure, there might not be a marble staircase leading to floors above—heck, there isn't even a second floor—but this is home to me.

I leave my boots by the door and flop onto my comfy couch. A few years ago, Tinker Bell had talked me into adopting her discarded flat screen when she moved into an apartment in Grimmwich with Thumbelina, Humpty Dumpty, and Godfather Death. I guess she felt a little sorry for me when she saw my puny place.

With no satellite reception this deep in the woods, a TV just sounded like a bad joke. Of course, I didn't tell her that. You should never hurt a pixie's feelings. Very bad idea, trust me. It was a nice gesture, though, so now the device just collects dust in the cellar until she notifies me of a visit—which isn't all too often, thank the fairies. That thing is darn heavy and quite cumbersome to carry up the stairs.

Lacking the common luxuries of the people in town, I pick up my alternative entertainment from the coffee table: *Harry Potter and the Prisoner of Azkaban*. The book is property of the Grimmwich Library and, yikes, that boy has a tough story to act out in his universe.

I skim through the volume to page 302 because that's where I stopped reading last night when the urge to go out and play with Jack set in. Scooting deeper into the cushions, I pull up my knees and lean the book against my thighs, starting with the first paragraph on that page. Oh, Harry, what kind of trouble did you get yourself into this time?

After the second paragraph, I close the book and put it back on the coffee table. The early afternoon sun shines like a bright smile through the window, right into my face. I get up and carefully pack a bottle of red wine and a marble cake into my neat, woven basket. An embroidered doily goes over it to cover the items from nosy birds or other hungry animals in the forest.

Slamming my shoes together outside helps shake off most of the dried dirt from earlier. I slip them back on, strap my bow and quiver to my back, close the door, and walk off along the narrow path through the trees that leads to Granny's. All the way, I hum a sweet tune from my childhood. Only when I start skipping, happily swinging the basket beside me, do I suddenly feel like I've done this all before and realize what the hell is going on.

Skittering to a stop, I lift my face to the sky and shout at the treetops, "Are you kidding me?!" Holy storybook, it hasn't even been twelve hours since I last walked that way and started the tale with Jack and Granny. They can't be serious, expecting me to act it out a second time today.

That I didn't notice what was happening straightaway isn't unusual. When the familiar pull of the story sets in, it's always hard to tell which are my real thoughts and which belong to the tale. There was one time I didn't figure out I was in the game until Jack snapped at me from Granny's bed and almost ripped my cloak apart.

That was a bit of a rude awakening.

Because the call is so very intense, the only thing I can

do is keep walking. But, dang it, I refuse to hum the stupid song and decide to meet Jack with a sinister expression instead. I know where to find him. Right down this path at the crossroads. He'll be leaning against the signpost, hands in the pockets of his leather jacket, one leg angled, and his foot flat against the pole. His dark eyes will glint through the wild, multihued strands of black and brown hair falling over his forehead as he watches me draw closer. He'll wait a few seconds, and then he'll crack a tiny, lopsided smile. Because he always does. He's done so for as long as I can remember.

Chapter 2

Jack

Llike the music in this pub. It's the reason I come here so often. For the band, the scotch, and to play pool with Phil and Eric.

My feet resting on the low bar of the stool, I bounce my right leg to the rhythm of the Town Musicians of Bremen, who perform their rock songs on a small stage at the back. The food's mostly a turn-off here, but they make good fries. I love fries. Wish I'd had some to go with Granny Redcoat this morning. With a bucket of ketchup. The old bag tastes like castor oil and porridge. Always a battle to stuff her down my throat.

I pick a fry from the basket on the bar that Tweedledee—or was it Tweedledum?—placed in front of me. Heck, I can never tell those two apart. Between a breath of the cigarette smoke and the stale odor of beer in the dimly lit place, I bite off the end of my fry.

"Whiskey and fries for breakfast?" The throaty laughter that follows accompanies a royal hand swiping some of my food. "Looks like you had a tough night."

I half turn my head to greet Phillip with a growl and then eat a little faster because I know he'll keep reaching into the basket until it's empty. Normally, I don't mind sharing, but today, I'm starving. "Get your own food, you son of a queen."

"Can't. I'm used to being fed," he retorts insolently, grinning around the stick in his mouth as he grabs a few more fries.

I push the basket to the other side, out of his reach. "Then go back to Castle Grove and have your girl cook you something nice."

My jacket draped over the bar stool next to me kept him a free seat. He tosses the leather on the counter then pulls the stool noisily closer and sits down. "*My* girl's hanging out with *your* girl at Jason's castle right now, and I don't think she can even make scrambled eggs."

An alarmed gasp makes us both turn around to a frozen Humpty with two glasses of Chardonnay in his pale hands. His eyes and mouth are three big *Os*.

It's funny how color always rises in Phillip's face when he accidentally treads on someone's toes. Tough guy or not, one's true fairy-tale traits are hard to shake off. "Sorry," my pal mumbles an apology to the flamboyant egg, rubbing his neck as we watch Humpty Dumpty flitter away with the drinks. As he takes a seat in a booth by the door with Christopher the Tooth Fairy, I return my focus to my meal.

"The regular princess meeting again?" I pick up the subject of earlier when Phil said something about our girls. Sure, Riley isn't *really* my girl. Not in the romantic sense. But officially, she is. Fairy tale law binds us closer together than a superficial ring on her finger ever could.

"Gossip girls, I'd rather call them." Phil snorts a chuckle and runs a hand through his fair hair before he orders a beer and then turns back to me. "They're undoubtedly trashing us from the first second 'til the last."

My teeth catching Riley's behind this morning is certainly something that she will bring up in front of her friends. I normally don't act out of my role. She was in such a cheeky mood today, though, permanently taunting me with her favorite name for me, that I couldn't resist reminding her what a nice set of fangs her *puppy dog* actually has.

A secretive sneer tugs at my lips. She really has a fine ass. I would love to get my teeth on it without her cloak in the way for once. I bet I could make her yip like a wolf.

I finish my fries, leaving three in the basket and

pushing them in front of Phillip. While he scarves them down, I dilute the salty taste on my tongue with a draught from the scotch and then wipe my mouth on the sleeve of my black *T.M.o.B.* band t-shirt. What can I say, I really dig these guys. Elbowing my friend, I point a thumb over to the pool table. "Care for a game?"

He nods, licking his fingers free of salt. We slide from our stools, head over, and I pull the release lever. A familiar rumble sounds from inside the table as the balls quickly roll down one after another into the removal window. Phillip sets them up in the black plastic triangle. In the meantime, I pick up a cue and rub the blue chalk over its tip. With a high toss, I throw the other cue at the prince.

He catches it one-handed and chalks it, too, when the sound of a well-known voice draws both of our gazes to the door. At long last, Eric comes into the pub with a half-dreamy, half-crazed look. The clock above the door says ten-thirty. Phillip steps in front of me with a mean smirk on his clean-shaven face as he rolls the sleeves of his red shirt up to the elbows. "Loser has to bring Eric home today."

That triggers my laugh. If Prince Eric joins us this late on a Sunday morning, it means his own story of *The Little Mermaid* held him up. The curse the Sea Witch casts on him shortly before the end of his tale badgers him so much that he usually gets wasted afterward to flush every remaining ounce of it from his body.

I take my half-empty glass from the bar and place it on

the edge of the pool table. Then I lean down with a grin and aim for my first shot. "Deal."

The balls scatter, the red one disappearing into the left corner pocket. Red is always the first one I dunk.

"Nice shot," Eric says in greeting and slumps onto the wooden chair by the small, round table close to us. He pours himself a glass of red wine from the bottle he picked up at the bar on his way over and knocks down the first half. Then he refills it, tips back with the chair, and stacks his booted feet on the table, swaying the glass in our direction. "Cheers."

I sink two more balls but miss the fourth shot. Damnit. While Phil has a go at the game, I take my scotch and sit down opposite Eric. We clink glasses and both take a sip—me a small one, him virtually inhaling his drink.

"Easy there, your royal highness," I mock him. "Don't want you to puke on my shoes later." And from the speed with which Phil sinks one ball after another, it's quite likely that I'll be the one taking the soon-to-be-drunk prince home today.

"I'll take it easy in the afternoon when I sleep off my inebriation," Eric replies with a snide grin and opens the top button of his white dress shirt. "As for now…" He lifts the wine bottle and calls to Merida, who waits tables here at the *Shady Wonders* during the week, "Darling, would you bring me another?"

The Highland beauty with the wild dark hair knows his habit as well as we do, so she doesn't even bother pointing out that the one he's holding is still half-full. Twenty seconds later, she places the new bottle in front of him, wipes her hands on her white apron, and then claps him softly on the shoulder, her face contorted in lines of sympathy. "Enjoy."

I grab a fistful of Merida's green linen dress before she can scurry away and lift my pleading gaze to her freckled face. "Can you bring him a double cheeseburger, too?" I know that Eric never gets to eat any of the cake at his own wedding. And for a drinking bout such as the one currently on his mind, some solid underlay couldn't hurt.

Eric throws me a look as if to say that I'm not his nanny, but drool practically seeps from the corner of his mouth at the prospect of some real food. From what we hear, Ariel is on a mission lately to turn him into a vegetarian. Oh, she can try, but I doubt she'll have any luck with it. Her only chance would be to blackmail him by refusing to... Yeah, well, let's just say she won't be lucky.

Phillip dunked five balls but missed his last shot, so we switch places. I empty the table of all colored balls except the black one, and when it's his turn again, of course he runs them all into the pockets one by one. "Good game," I compliment him and throw a glance at our pal, who's getting sloshed quicker than is good for him. That's going to be an interesting walk to his castle later.

Phil and I play a few more games, slowly drinking as we do. But when Eric dips forward, pillowing his head on one arm, the other one hanging listlessly at his side as he begins to snore, the fun is over. "Time to take his highness home and tuck him in," Phillip jokes, putting his cue away. Thank Grimm, the black-haired prince doesn't have to act his role all too often these days. The Sea Witch's curse would be shit compared to the alcoholic cirrhosis he'd end up giving himself.

I place my cue back on the stand and toss the money for my drinks and the fries onto the bar, adding a tip for whichever of the Tweedles served me. Then I put on my jacket and join Phil by Eric. "Come on, Sleeping Beauty," I say, hauling him up by slipping my bulk under his shoulder. Phillip takes his other arm, and together, we walk him outside. The moans coming from Eric prove that he's still alive.

Phillip's topless coach with the two gorgeous, white horses is parked in front of the pub. As we stop there, he hesitates a moment, patting Eric's cheek rather roughly. "You okay, boy?"

"Uh-huh," the raspy answer drifts from his hanging head.

Taking him home with the cabriolet would be way faster than dragging the semi-conscious prince down to his palace by the shore. But I can see why Phillip doesn't want Eric to ride with him. Last time we did that, he threw up. No matter how often Phil's servants cleaned the cushions, the stench remained, and it was pestilent. Ultimately, he had to get a new coach.

I'm preparing to support the boozehound's whole

weight so Phillip can get free, except a rather persistent pull toward the Wood of 1000 Dawns sets in right then and brings on a change of plans.

"Sorry, but Eric is your job today," I apologize and wrap the drunken prince's arm around Phillip's shoulders.

Phil stares at me wide-eyed as he has a fully grown man hanging around his neck and holds him tight like a dead wife. "Why?"

"Date with Riley." I smack him on the shoulder and grin halfheartedly.

"Again?"

Some stories are told more often than others. Phillip and Aurora usually have to act theirs out once every few days. Ariel and Eric often get a few weeks between their plays most of the time. Riley and I, on the other hand, front-run Fairyland's most-wanted list. We hardly get a day off. But playing twice in twenty-four hours is rare, even for us.

Roguishly, I waggle my brows at Phil and his accessory. A rendezvous with Red Riding Hood is the better end of this deal—for so many reasons.

Sure, it means leaving my best friend to fight the battle with Eric alone when he actually won the game of pool, but he knows that none of us can resist the mystical call when someone in The Reality reads the words *Once upon a time…*

Phil rolls his eyes and then starts laughing. "Screw you, Jack. If you made this up to bail, I'm going to kick your ass down to Eldorado."

Lifting my hands, I put a solemn expression on my face. "Not bailing, I swear." He has seen me taking Eric home on many occasions. I'm not one to escape from a job when it's about friends. But the story always comes first.

"I only believe you because I know you can't fake that gleam in your eyes when it's about Red Riding Hood. But you owe me, dude."

That glimmer is not intentional. It comes from the wolf part of me. There's this deep, annoying need inside me to just nibble Riley up. Heck, if she ever lets me.

"Next time, Eric is my duty again. Promise. You know"—I scratch my head—"you could make him throw up here and then bring him home in your runabout. By the way…" I point a finger at Eric's face pillowed against Phillip's chest. "He's drooling on your shirt."

Disgusted, Phil shifts him a little in his grip and considers my suggestion for a couple of seconds. In the end, he shakes his head. "Nah. A little walk and some fresh air will do him some good. See ya! And tell your girl I said hi."

I nod. "Take care!"

We part in front of the pub and head in opposite directions. The pull is getting stronger, irresistible, and it carries with it the excitement of seeing Riley again. I know I'll never get to have my way with her, not in our story setup, but the ties to our tale are sometimes seriously hard to cut out of my mind and system.

As I leave the village far behind and cross the borders of the Wood of 1000 Dawns, I sneer at a doe with her fawn in the underbrush and then give a deep, guttural growl to make them dart off in terror…just because I can.

It's not far to the crossroads, our usual meeting place. As always, I'm the first to arrive. Hands in my jacket pockets, I lean against the signpost that points to Grimmwich, Granny's House, the Plush Toy Forest, and Glitter Hollow. The latter is the direction from which Riley will appear in a few minutes. Inhaling deeply and filtering the air through my nose, I can already smell her. Damn, I dig the mix of morning dew and wood strawberries.

With my hypersensitive hearing, thanks to the wolf part of me, I can hear her footsteps, too. Oddly, there's no humming today.

A chuckle escapes me. Ooh, someone's peeved. This is going to be interesting.

Angling one leg and planting the sole of my shoe against the post behind me, I lower my chin but keep an eye on the path in front of me. She's close, I can sense her. A hot feeling enters my gut and makes the hair on my neck stand on end. It's always the same at the beginning of our adventure.

Time to brace myself. The first sight usually triggers the impulse in me to change into the big, bad Wolf and just have a go at this girl. It's immediately followed by a much deeper need to do other things with her. Sinful things. I've been trying to lure her off the righteous path and seduce her into a realm of no shame and regret for as long as I can remember.

But she never comes.

Pity. It would take a fool not to notice her innocent beauty; her tempting curves, which most of the time are hidden under her cloak. But I am no fool, and that shy look only she can master at every first smile I give her is my downfall.

Of course, this is all just part of the story.

Even if I have to admit that I thought about hooking up with Riley when we were first thrown into the same tale. She shot me down. Maybe I shouldn't have asked her out on a date right after eating her grandma for the first time.

She never gave me a second chance, and I never asked for one either. There are other girls in town to scratch a certain itch. Gretel has been good company for a while, and she never stayed over when we were done—which I appreciated. As for Riley, I don't need to put a ring on her finger or take her to my bed. Because there's one thing she can never change. She's my girl, and she will be forever.

Bush-wood rustles in the distance and puts me on alert.

Five…four…three… She's just around the bend. A smile begins to tug at the corners of my mouth. Two…one… Here she comes.

Chapter 3

Riley

As I near the giant oak before the last bend, a round of robins rises from the tree and circles the crown. Magic is in the air… It always is when the robins fly in circles. And the magic they're announcing waits just around the corner. Jack.

The wolf part of him makes him a special character here in Fairyland. We have all kinds of magical creatures: mermaids, witches, fairies, and elves. Farther in the East, there's a vampire who hides in a castle during the daytime, and several shapeshifters hang out in the surrounding forests, too. I might stand out from the crowd with my shiny, red cloak, but other than that, I'm nothing special. Not like *him*. I couldn't turn into a freaking mouse if my life depended on it.

But Jack is really good at what he does. He can shift shapes back and forth as often he wants. The huge, autumn-colored wolf with snow and sand streaks marking his fur is quite a sight. Even though he's not allowed to eat me in our story, I like to keep my distance from him. One can never know when a wild animal will suddenly snap and start seeing you as a fine knuckle of pork.

I clasp the basket for Granny a little tighter in front of my belly and bravely lift my chin as I take the last few steps that bring me in sight of the big, bad Wolf. Even though I know exactly what to expect, a tiny shiver of fear zips through my body as our gazes lock for the first time in this new rendition of our story.

Big? Yeah. Jack is a head taller than me.

Bad? Oh, yes! You don't need to know him personally to perceive the danger he breaths out.

Wolf? Not yet. And still, my steps falter.

"Good afternoon, little Miss Red Riding Hood," he purrs, tilting his head just slightly.

His dark eyes sparkle eerily in the beams of light sifting through the trees. The corners of his mouth lift. For the briefest second, I don't know whether to smile back or run away. He always triggers this strange reaction in me, in spite of me having this tale down pat. It's like a reflex I can't turn off, not even after so many years. But it's gone the moment I remember why I'm here. Second play today. And I'm still mad at him.

Three steps separate us. Normally, I'd stop by him so he can try to lure me to the dark parts of the forest. Not that he's ever had any luck before. Today, I don't care for our routine little chat. I want this tale over and done with. Fast. Harry Potter is waiting for me in my cozy hut.

Jaw set and lips pressed together, I pull up my hood and stalk past him, continuing on the path to Granny's house. He can hang there and wait for the White Rabbit to have a chat with him for all I care.

Jack laughs out behind me. "Riley! Come back!"

"No."

"Please…"

Oh, dang it. I hate when he sounds like a poor puppy because he plays it so well. But he won't stop me. Not this time. "You can bi—" A startled gasp escapes me. Suddenly, I'm whirled around, and the basket slips from my hand, tumbling to the mossy ground.

My back hits a tree trunk, and Jack presses his body flush to mine. I can feel his breath inside my hood as he snarls into my ear, "Say it, and I'll do it."

Goodness, telling a wolf to bite you is so not a smart idea. What was I thinking?

In memory of this morning's encounter with his teeth, I rub the side of my butt, which he doesn't miss. His gaze drops to my hip and then moves back up to my face. "Still hurting?" he murmurs through a salacious smirk and lets his hand slide down to my side.

What the freak? This is not how our play should run. Angry, I push at his chest. "Get off me and go find yourself a squirrel to play with. I don't want to talk to you."

He lets me move him, but not too far. Only a few inches back. At the same time, his right arm shoots out, and he braces his hand next to my head on the tree, blocking my escape. "You know it's not working like this." His other hand moves up to my face, and he softly strokes his knuckles across my cheek. Then he carefully brushes back my hood and dips his forehead to mine, capturing my eyes with his. "So, be a nice girl, and let's have some fun."

Chills rush through me as I draw in a breath. In all our time, Jack has never touched me like this. It feels…strange. Not uncomfortable. He's never looked at me like this either, and oddly enough, it's hard to look away. What in the world is up with him?

"Jack…" I whisper. And suddenly, I notice the sharp smell on his breath. My brows furrow, my voice immediately gaining strength again. "Are you drunk?"

He leans in to my ear, his dark stubble rubbing gently against my skin. "Just a little bit," he murmurs quietly and nips my earlobe. The sharp sting coaxes a tiny squeak from me, which makes him chuckle. "So, will you come into the shadows with me now?"

Jack Wolf has never once come to work drunk.

I don't know what he goes off and does after we finish

our tale each time, but he takes his job seriously. He's always at the meeting point when I arrive. He usually makes it easy for me to escape his ensnarement at the beginning. And he never hesitates to swallow Granny, even though I know how scared he is of the moment when the Huntsman comes to free her.

Sure, neither of us imagined we'd be meeting a second time here today, and what he does in his spare time is none of my business, but it's weird to get a glimpse of his private life for once. I wonder what he had to drink. Does he prefer vodka? Whiskey? Beer? I don't drink at all so I wouldn't know the difference. It must have been more than one glass, though. Otherwise, he wouldn't be behaving so strangely.

A very tempting thought crosses my mind. Since we're already wandering off the lines of the tale, why not go a little further? What if we…say…slightly alter the plot?

Whatever answer Jack expected from me to continue our usual story—and what was certainly on my tongue a moment ago—is gone now. My stunned expression fades as determination rises within me. I close my half-parted mouth, my heart beating a reckless rhythm. Then I bite my lip and dare a deep look into Jack's dark and dangerous eyes. "Okay…"

He blinks. Slowly. "What?"

My gaze doesn't waver, and it probably takes on an excited and hopeful note as a small smile creeps across my face. "Okay… I'll come into the shadows with you."

Jack takes a step back and fixes me with narrowed eyes. "Are you crazy?"

His reaction hurts me after ten thousand first encounters where he always wanted to seduce me off the right path. A pout replaces my adventurous grin. "No. I'm just tired of playing this stupid tale over and over again. Aren't you? Always going the same way, always facing a bloody end? And never getting kissed in all this time."

Now his forehead creases even more. "You want to get kissed?"

"Well…*yeah*." I cross my arms over my chest. "All my friends have love stories to play. They're happy and totally romanced-up…ish. Sort of." Resolutely, I lift my chin. "I want that, too."

Jack's usually determined face scrunches up further as he shifts his weight from one foot to the other. "And you want that with me?" His gaze sweeps past me into the trees and back. "Over there, in the shadows?"

"No, silly!" I roll my eyes. "Of course, *not*."

"*Of course,* not," he repeats my words on a growl as if I hurt his feelings beyond repair. Playing all these years has certainly turned him into a devilishly good actor.

"For your information," I tell him solemnly with my head held high, "I want to catch myself a prince."

And that cracks him up. "You want what?" he barks in laughter, tucking his hands into his jeans' pockets.

I throw him a pissy glare and snarl, "Yeah, get a grip, puppy dog." Should I have seen this fit coming? Probably.

Still, it won't hold me back. I've made up my mind, and we're going to get through this, whether or not he finds the idea ridiculous.

I stride to the bush where my basket rolled earlier when he grabbed me and put the fallen bottle of wine back inside. Jack still stands in the middle of the path, staring at me as if I'd turned into a three-headed dragon. I walk past him, in the opposite direction of Granny's house, expecting him to follow me. He doesn't.

"Are you coming or not?" I snap over my shoulder.

A moment ticks by before he moves and catches up with me. His voice still holds a thread of doubt. "Where to?"

"For starters, to the dark parts of the woods. Where are they?"

"I don't know."

I stop and whirl around to him. "You don't *know*?!" Outraged, I throw my hands with the basket in the air. "You've been trying to lure me there for ages. Where did you think we'd go if I finally said *yes*?"

"I knew you wouldn't, so there wasn't a need to think about it." His eyes are dark again and drained of all amusement. His voice heats up, though, just like mine.

"You're a wolf. Don't you eternally roam this place, sniffing rabbit tracks and marking trees? You should know the forest like the back of your hand."

"I live in an apartment above Geppetto's workshop in the village," he growls at me from the side. "I only come here to play with you."

"Just great." Chuffing, I stride on, picking the path to the Plush Toy Forest for now. At least there's something that might help me find what I want.

Jack reads the sign pointing out the direction, and his temper eases to curiosity again. "You want to visit the three bears?"

"No. I don't think they'll be much help." Pulling up my hood, I cast him a contemplative, sideways glance from under the red fabric and grin again because my idea is genius. "Cupid's tree is there, too."

Everyone knows about the specialty of that tree, but from the way Jack bites the inside of his cheek, he doesn't seem to have any idea what we'll do there. Good. He'd probably try to stop me if he knew.

At the sound of running water ahead, a queasy feeling grips me. Flowing backward from the sea to its well in the Marble Mountains, the Timeless Brook cuts a swath through the Wood of 1000 Dawns, separating all stories into sections of sorts. Our path continues over a little, wooden bridge. As we near it, hesitation creeps into Jack's pace. I know what's holding him back—I can feel the tug of our story, too. It wants us to turn back and continue what we're meant to do. Even the basket in my hand starts trembling, pulling at my arm as if it wants to shout that Granny's house is in the opposite direction.

I grip the handle tighter and stop in front of the bridge, daring a glance up at Jack's face. He's silently staring at the border between the bridge and land. "Are you afraid?" I whisper, not knowing if the question is really for him or myself. What will happen if we really cross that stream? No one has ever dared to break out of their tale before. At least none who ever came back to tell the story.

Jack's eyes move to my side, but the rest of him remains motionless. There's a hint of wariness in his gaze. "And you?"

I swallow. Hell, yes, I am. But if I don't do this now, I'll never get my happily ever after. So I draw in a deep breath, bravely holding his stare, and then straighten my back. "No." And with that one little word, I take a step forward and walk onto the bridge.

It supports me, not breaking from shock and dumping me into the river with a splash. *Phew.* For a second there, I really wasn't sure. But with my next step, the basket slips out of my hand, shooting off. "What the—" As I spin around, I find that it zoomed right into Jack's arms. A low, whiny sound emerges from it.

"You made it cry," Jack says, faking a scrunched, sympathetic face, cuddling the basket to his chest as if it was a baby wolf. "I'm sure it wants to fly off to your grandma's house. It's scared of running away."

With a snort, I stride back to him and rip the thing out of his arms. "It's only a basket! Don't whack out here." I pull off the doily and hold out a piece of the cake I put in there before I left home. "See? Just normal food and wine." To prove my point, I take a bite. Next thing I know, the sky above the treetops rapidly darkens with clouds, and thunder rolls in from all sides.

Holy pot of gold at the end of the rainbow!

"Riley?"

My gaze snaps from the upset sky to an even more upset Jack.

"You better put that cake back into the basket and bring it to your granny."

I hesitate. "If I do that, we'll have the same stupid conversations every freaking day from now until forever." More determination enters my voice. "And I'll never find romance."

His insistent gaze pleads with me. "There are worse things."

"Really? You don't mind getting your belly cut open by the Huntsman each time at the end of our story?"

He waits a beat to answer, but his severe expression doesn't falter. "I'm used to it. I can bear it."

"Yeah? Because I can't," I snap at him. "I want more from my life."

Jack holds out his hand. "Give it to me."

"No." I back a step away from him.

His eyes get so dark I think I can see the night sky in them as he yells, "Give me that damn cake, Riley!"

His demand is so compelling, he almost drags me toward him with invisible cords. But I cannot do that. We've gone too far to turn around now. This is my chance. *Our* chance. So with a determined glare, I stuff the entire piece of cake into my mouth, filling my cheeks until I can't even chew the darn thing.

At the increasing rumbles of thunder, Jack drops to a squat in a wild panic and throws his arms over his head. Thankfully, no lightning shoots down on us. Hah! Is that all they have in store? The basket still in one hand, I spread my arms and lift my head to the sky. Crumbs of cake spew out of my mouth as I yell, "Now what? I'm not going back, so what will you do, huh?"

Almost choking on the dry clump in my mouth, I salivate it to mush until I can finally swallow. Boy, that thing went down hard. I pat my chest, coughing up a few remaining crumbs. When the coughing fit is over, so is the thunder. I only notice because Jack is kneeling in a beam of sunlight again instead of cloudy shadows. He dares a glance upward before he straightens back to his full, imposing height.

"See?" I say confidently and cast him a triumphant smile. "That wasn't the end of the world." Another bout of crumbs tickles my throat, so I reach into the basket and take out the wine. With my teeth, I pull out the cork and spit it over the bridge railing, into the water. But before the first drop of wine can touch my tongue, Jack rushes forward and yanks the bottle out of my hand.

"No, don't!" he shouts, holding the liquor away from me. "You've never been drinking before, have you?"

"No…" My brows fall into a V because I don't see his point. "Why?"

"Because I don't want you to do"—he furiously waves his arms around him—"whatever we're setting out to do here, drunk." Then he rakes a desperate hand through his messy, multihued hair. I bet if he could, he'd turn tail and run off home now. But how would that look coming from the big, bad Wolf? Chickening out when a mere, weak girl is holding her ground? He looks first at me and then at the bottle. In the end, *he* takes a deep draught from it. I don't know if he does it to calm himself or if he's just trying to eliminate the stuff so I don't get any. But when his gaze falls to the empty basket in my hand, he releases a helpless sigh. A hint of surrender appears in his eyes as they find mine. Then he throws the bottle off the bridge and into the water. It bobs up and down as the stream carries it away.

For an infinite moment, we both just stand there on the wooden bridge and look at each other. Then we turn to the other shore where the Plush Toy Forest stretches out before us.

"You'll get us in trouble," Jack says, finally capitulating to my plan.

I offer him a bright smile. "And you're scared of trouble *since when?*"

Mischief gleams in his eyes as the left side of his mouth tilts up, and he snorts. I knew he wouldn't be able to resist a provocation like this. Filled with a wave of excitement, I toss the basket after the bottle, grab Jack's hand, and pull him along with me into a whole new adventure.

Chapter 4

Jack

She's cute when she's excited. I never noticed that before. It's the only reason why I give in and following Riley to the other section of the forest. The Plush Toy Forest is dangerous ground. Too many bears and bunnies live here. Since the call of our own story already started, it won't be long until the wolf in me wants out, needing to satiate its hunger. I guess it wouldn't be that big of a deal to gobble the middle one of the three little pigs. There'd still be the bricklayer and another one left. But if a certain piglet or a delicious yellow bear crosses our path at the wrong time, things could take an unpleasant turn in Fairyland.

I'd rather avoid that and get back in time to finish our play. Old Mrs. Redcoat is probably waiting for her cake, too. She won't be happy to find out that Riley stuffed the entire thing down her throat. A smile pulls on my mouth at the memory of her bulging chipmunk cheeks when she ate it. Crazy girl. I didn't know she could be this reckless.

"So, what do you want from Cupid?" I ask as we stroll through the picturesque wood. She's still holding my hand, tugging me along as if she's worried I might change my mind and take off in the other direction. *Well, honeydrop, if I did, you'd be hanging over my shoulder and coming along, too. Promise.* No chance I'm going back without her. In fact, I'm only waiting for her to realize what a harebrained mission she's put us on and come to her senses. We won't be able to deny our roles for too long. The situation will turn nasty if we do.

"From Cupid?" She looks at me in exhilaration, not slowing down a bit. "Nothing. And I really hope he's not around when we reach his tree."

Now she has my guts in a curious twist. When she said that she wanted romance and mentioned the dwarf-angel in diapers with his magical bow and arrow, I thought she might have heard of a way to shake up our story a bit. Whether the fluttering little guy can really do something like that, I'm not sure. Maybe if there was an official, legitimate hearing with the great storyteller. But, frankly, I've never heard of anyone ever actually meeting that ghostly voice of the tales. For all we know, he might just be a myth.

"Going to steal a few apples from his tree?" I joke because I can't imagine what else Riley would be so eager to find out here.

"Not apples..." Her rakish gaze meets mine from under her hood as the forest clears in front of us. We reach a sunlit meadow with a single, huge, lush green tree in the very middle. "Just some twigs."

"Twigs?" I laugh. "What do you want with—?" The words die in my throat. I pull her to an abrupt stop, whirling her around to face me. "Wait. You're not going to—"

"You bet!" Her delicate hand slips from mine, and she props both of them on her hips. "I have a right to romance. And if I have to take it into my own hands, I will."

"This tree is magical. It's forbidden to break twigs or branches from it. I'm not even sure you're allowed to touch it." I gesture down her body. "Unless you've got a set of wings stored under that cloak that I don't know about."

"When exactly did you change into a square, puppy dog?" she mocks me. "I know people who know people who tell stories about you... And your reputation speaks for itself."

The hypocrisy isn't lost on me. When have I ever let someone stop me from doing something forbidden? On the other hand, it's not funny to get chased down by angry villagers with pitchforks that want to skin you alive. In fact,

I've been happy to keep a low profile for years. Besides, this is about the girl I've been playing out a tale with since the beginning of time. I'm not sure I like that she's going to make severe changes to what we have.

"I'm the mean Wolf in this tale, remember? I'm meant to be bad. You're…*sweet little Red Riding Hood*." I emphasize the last words to make my point clear.

Riley contemplates that for a long moment. Her face stays stoic, her hard gaze never wavering from mine. Until she suddenly lifts on her toes, leans in very close, and slowly whispers in my ear, "Chicken."

An annoyed growl emanates from my throat. The girl obviously needs a private lesson in the kind of animal she's dealing with here. With a tight grip on her waist, I pull her in fast and snarl in her face, "If I wasn't afraid to eat you alive, I'd let the Wolf out right now to settle this argument once and for all."

A small gasp of surprise breaks free from her slightly parted lips, and she shoves at my chest. But the first second of shock fades, and a snide gleam enters her gaze. "Don't go macho Wolf on me here. Rather, come and help me break off a couple branches instead."

I don't even have time to utter a reply because she's clasping my hand and pulling me toward the giant tree in the wake of her ever-so-sprightly stride. *What the hell—* Why do I let this girl command me around so much of late? No one has ever shot me down like she just did.

Then again, it feels strange to be with her outside of

our tale. Each of our lines has been set in stone. There hasn't been the smallest deviance. Ever. I've known this girl—her every move and word—by heart for what seems like forever. Now, for the first time in so many years, I don't know what to expect from her.

Confusion locks my tongue down as I let her drag me across the luscious, green meadow. She's like the young, spirited *puppy dog* she loves calling me so much.

Riley stops beneath the tree and takes off her bow and quiver to lean them against the trunk. Then she tilts her face up to gape at the overhanging branches. They're a little too high for her to reach. The realization spawns a sigh. *Well, bad luck, little girl.* I guess she'll have to drop the crazy idea now, and we can finally head back.

Or… She releases the single button of her cloak at her throat and takes it off.

"Mmm, stripping?" Now things are getting interesting. "Go on," I tease her with a smirk, leaning back against the tree and watching her, my arms and ankles crossed.

"No, not stripping." She cuts me a sharp glare and then throws the bundled cloak at my face. I pull the red thing off my head and clasp it. Riley also takes off her shoes and then stalks toward me barefoot. Facing off, I have no idea what will come next from her. But I wonder…

"Lift me."

Her words derail my thoughts. I'm speechless for a second. "What?"

"Help me up," she orders. "I need to break off some good branches."

I tilt my head and arch one eyebrow. "You're kidding me, right?"

"Well, I can't climb this tree alone." Her gaze goes from commanding to helpless and innocent in under three seconds. "You're strong, and you're tall. I need your help. Please, Jack."

I don't know how she does it, but next thing I know, I toss the cloak aside, lace my fingers and, lips compressed, slightly bend my knees so she can place her little, warm foot into my hands. Holding on to my shoulders, she nods, and I ease her up.

"Higher, Jack," she demands. There's only so much I can do for her, but she finds her way. Getting a hold of my hair, she places one knee on my shoulder, the second one following on the other side as her skirt swallows me up.

"Riley," a deep, raspy groan escapes me when my head ends up between her thighs all of a sudden, my nose just an inch away from the red scrap of satin that is her panties. Screwed treasure of a leprechaun, does she even know what she's doing to me?

I imagine not when her command, "Hold still, I'm almost there," comes from outside the red-tinted spell she's put me under. Behind closed lids, I roll my eyes, praying for enough self-control to get through this without doing something stupid.

As she works her way up to stand on my shoulders, I

keep a hold of her ankles so she won't fall off. Her skin is warm and smooth under my fingers. Tempting. Slowly, I push my hands up higher, sliding them over her shins and calves. Damn, Riley feels like forbidden silk. Stuck between her legs, my gaze moves up completely of its own accord. The reward is a glimpse into Eden. Above my face, there's the enticing red apple waiting to be plucked.

"Jack! Are you feeling me up?" a girlish huff sounds from above.

My hands stop where they are. "No."

One palm braced on the tree for support, she bends down, gathering and tucking the dress between her thighs, and scowls into my still tilted-up face. "Don't gawk under my skirt, Wolf!"

I crack a lecherous grin. "Then stop fooling around in the tree and come down!"

"In a moment. When I have—" Because she obviously doesn't want to let go of her dress and needs the other hand to grab whatever she has her eyes on up there, she starts to wobble on my shoulders. Even with the tight grip I have on her thighs now, I can't balance her for long.

"Riley, come down!" I growl.

A squeak, her dress fanning out again, wood breaking, and the next second, she drops into my arms. She's light as a feather, cushy to hold. Her face, a little flushed from fright, is now covered by a couple of stray locks. I blow them away for her and glare darkly into her eyes.

"Oops." She eyes me sheepishly. Then her rosy lips

stretch into a proud smile as she holds out one stick in either hand.

I put her back on her feet, quickly glancing around and hoping that nobody saw what we just did while she slips back into her shoes. We're still alone, thank Grimm. "Now what?" I demand, my scolding gaze back on her. "You want to smack someone over the head with them?"

Returning my glare with determination, Riley sinks onto a rock in the longish grass close to the tree and surprises me when she pulls out a pocketknife from her right boot. "Now, I make an arrow." She unfolds the blade and starts sharpening one end of the straight stick. "And instead of throwing your useless jokes around, you can help me with this." Obviously impatient with my lack of enthusiasm for her mission, she gets to her feet again, stalks over, and pushes the second love branch forcefully against my chest. "I'm assuming you have a knife. Or aren't puppy dogs allowed to play with sharp things?"

Ugh. How does she always know which buttons to push to get what she wants? I grasp the stick and get out my own knife which, unlike her, I keep in my pocket. We settle down on the rock that is big enough for both of us and silently go to work.

Every now and then, I peek over at her to follow up on how incredibly good she is at handcrafting the weapon. "So, what are you going to do with them once they're finished?" I murmur after a while.

"Shoot me a prince, of course."

I lift an eyebrow. "And then live with him happily ever after?"

"Mm-hmm." All her anger has smoked off, and she's just eagerly at work now. "You know Grimm was a bastard for not writing me into a beautiful, romantic story. So I'll just have to take things into my own hands now."

Damn, I thought she was only joking when she talked about finding a prince for herself. Now, an awkward feeling twists my stomach. She can't really do this, right? I mean, our story is carved in stone. She can't just replace me with a different ever after. What will become of me if she slips into another tale? I'm the big, bad Wolf. There aren't too many options for someone like me in Fairyland. I can either start blowing the three little pigs' houses down, or take up a role in Peter and the Wolf. But Peter is… Well, shit, I don't want to play with Peter.

Riley starts working the back end of her arrow by cutting a thin slit and sliding in a couple of small leaves for fletching feathers. When she's done, she crosses to the tree to get her bow and draws it for a test. It looks good. Way too good. Actually, it looks as if it really might function for the purpose it was made for.

Done with my own arrow, I stand up and walk toward her, twisting the stick through my fingers. A gloomy edge enters my voice. "Do you even know how it works? Where you have to hit your prince to make him fall in love with you?"

"I'll just aim at his heart." Her spirited grin and

lighthearted mood back in place, she turns to me with the bow drawn and points the arrow straight at my chest.

I stop the stick-twisting. A dangerous growl escapes me. "Bad idea, honeydrop." With two fingers, I push the tip of her weapon away. "We don't want that to accidentally go off."

She laughs, stepping back and raising the arrow again. Same target. "Why not? Afraid of feeling a little love for someone?"

Oh, Red Riding Hood wants to play? Let's make sure she really understands the rules then. "If you shoot this at me, you're the only person around that I *could* fall in love with." My chin dipped low and my eyes focused on her, I walk toward her with a slow, predatory stride. "So, tell me, little Riley…do you really want a lovesick wolf on your ass?"

Realization of the danger she's toying with finally glistens in her eyes. But it doesn't unhinge her reckless smile. She backs away from me slowly, my heart still in the line of fire. "Ooh, a cute little puppy—*whoa*!" Her feet get tangled in the red puddle of fabric behind her, and the arrow zooms off as she tumbles to the ground.

Thanks to devilishly fast reflexes, I catch the stick one-handed right before the sharp end drills through my skin. Mere pressure from my thumb breaks this one, and Riley's mouth falls open as she watches. Apparently, it's time to teach Red Riding Hood a lesson.

I toss the two ends away, not letting the brat on the

ground out of my sight. With a very slow prowl, I change into the Wolf, feeling the warm grass beneath my four paws as I move on. Still motionless on her back, her eyes widen in shock. I know why. She's never, *ever* seen me do this. As I step right over her, I bare my teeth at her face and puff a steamy breath against her skin, my snout a mere inch from her nose.

And now…beg for your life, little girl.

My wolf face reflects in her huge, frightened eyes. Her cheeks are pale, and her breathing is shaky. Yep, that's exactly the reaction I wanted. But then she blinks a couple of times, and a seriously cute smile dispels her scared expression. "I'm sorry, Jack."

No. I won't excuse this!

Warily, she reaches out and starts rubbing behind my ear. What the hell? I want to snap at her hand—carefully, of course, so I don't hurt her—but her fingers there in my fur work magic. Damn, that feels *good.* She tickles the spot and, suddenly, all I can do is squeeze my eyes shut in utter surrender.

My knees start to buckle. *Yeah, that's it. Right there, baby. A little more.* I sink into the long grass beside her and rest my head on my paws, groaning dreamily.

Riley sits up and continues the pleasure. Quietly, she giggles. "You like that?"

My eyes snap open. Shit! I shift back with a final snarl and get to my feet. "No." Patting the dirt off my clothes, I throw her a warning look. "And stop shooting arrows at me!"

Holy flea circus! What turned me into that fuzzy ball of no control? Using the moment when Riley gets up, I briefly shake myself so she can't see it. That was crazy. Until today, no one has ever touched me in wolf form. Apart from the Huntsman, but his touches are never those of great pleasure—and he always has a knife on him. As Riley throws the cloak around her shoulders and fastens it at the base of her throat, I narrow my eyes at her, scowling. This girl is sneaky, finding all the right spots to undo me.

I need a drink. Without a word, I head off across the meadow to the line of trees because I know a shortcut to the village. She follows me after she picks up the remaining, intact arrow. With a taunting smile pasted on her lips, she straps the bow and quiver to her back as she skips along beside me. "Where are we going now?"

"Pub. I'm done."

"What? *No!*" Her happy expression falls, and she grabs my arm to stop me. "Come on, Jack, let's give it a try first." She clasps the collar of my shirt and hauls herself up on her toes so her hopeful face is level with mine. "Please. We've come this far today. Let's find a prince and shoot him. See if this arrow really works."

I frown. "Well, if not, you'll be the new death-bringer of Fairyland. No more worries about romance then."

"So are you coming?"

We stare into each other's eyes for a lengthy moment. Her irises gleam like two drops of honey in the sun. And suddenly, I understand why I haven't eaten this girl all these years. She has me on toast. It's her eyes, her innocent look. She does that hopeful eyebrow-quirk thing, and I turn to complete putty in her hands. Fuck. When did that happen?

I wrap my fingers around hers and gently move them away from my shirt. "Mmrrrr…yyyyyes." Irritated with myself, I roll my eyes. "After all, if you shoot a prince dead, someone should be there to dispose of the corpse. And I missed my granny meal today."

"Oh, Jack, you're the best!" Exultation in her skipping step, she dashes off a few feet ahead, her red cloak flapping in the wind and looking just as happy as she does. Then she stops and turns expectantly. I can't share her enthusiasm, sorry. She'll have to settle for my moody pace.

Surprisingly, she does—without complaint. But when she walks on beside me, the excited tremor in her is still tangible. Riley is like a bouncy ball of fluffy unicorn laughter today. How one person can be this lively is beyond me. And yet, it raises a tiny smile.

After a few more steps, I cast a look down at her and cock an amused brow. "You always this jumpy outside our tale?"

Instead of giving me an answer, I can see how she's struggling to calm down. To no avail. In the end, her bright beam finds its way to my face. "I guess so." She clings to the string of her bow running across her chest and bounds a few steps ahead again, then comes back.

Excitedly, her hands wrap around my arm. "Just imagine, tonight I could find my happily ever after. We'll go out, he'll propose to me, and at the end of the story, we'll have a beautiful wedding inside his palace." Her eyes grow like sunflowers in the summer. "Wouldn't that be a gorgeous ending?"

The only *ending* I can see is me playing a role in Peter and the Wolf, and a hoard of angry village people chasing after me with pitchforks in the final quarter. So, no. That wouldn't be *gorgeous*.

The forest gets thinner around us again. This must be Kansas because I can see where the tornado left a swathe of fallen trees behind. One lies in our path, and I help Riley over it. Dorothy's house stands in the open space to our left, but that's not where we want to go, Riley informs me. Ahead is another signpost, toward which my red bouncy ball drags me. "Camelot?" I read out loud.

"Yes. They have King Arthur. His wife ran off with his first knight so he's alone again, right?" Her lips stretch wide. "Perfect for me."

"Ah, so becoming a princess in a cozy castle isn't enough anymore?" I laugh. "You want a whole kingdom to rule over."

"Not really," she replies meekly after a moment of deep thinking. "But he's the only single royal in Fairyland that I know of. I don't want to steal somebody else's prince." Then her face lights up a bit more again. "And he's hot from what I saw in *The Character Magazine*."

"Hot, huh?"

"Yeah. Like really handsome, you know?" She steps on a rock and ruffles my hair, grinning, and then tickles the spot she rubbed before when I was the Wolf. "Not like ragged, little puppy dogs."

Did she really just do that? I narrow my eyes to fake a mean scowl and sneer at her. "Run…little girl."

When a playful growl rumbles from my chest, Riley dashes away, squealing like a happy, young child. I chase her, but not in wolf form. That would be too easy. And too dangerous. Near a little brook barring our way, I catch up with my girl in red and grab her from behind. A surprised half-gasp, half-laugh escapes from her. Not wanting to fall into the runlet, I take off with her and jump across the water. On the other side, we topple down, Riley breaking her fall with my body.

She laughs so hard in my arms that she can barely manage to climb off me. The sound is interesting—and cute. Like the snicker of the purple My Little Pony. For a strangely long moment, it makes me just look at her. Still in the hold of the odd emotion, I reach up and wipe a tear of laughter from the corner of her eye with my thumb.

Her face feels incredibly soft, and suddenly, I want to know more about this girl that I only thought I knew for so long. The side she's showing me today is completely new. Curiosity takes over. I bring my thumb to my mouth and lick the small drop off.

Riley's laughter turns into an incredulous giggle. Still

lying on top of me, she slaps me on the shoulder. "Ew, Jack. That's gross."

No, it's not. It tastes delicious.

"Your tears are like sun-kissed honey," I honestly tell her with a smile. "I should make you cry more and make a drink from them."

"You're crazy." She laughs again, her hood sliding farther down her forehead to cover her twinkling eyes and half of her nose. Suddenly, all I see in front of me is a pair of sensual, rosy lips. I wonder what she'd do if I plucked a kiss from them. She said she wanted to be kissed, didn't she? And a kiss is a kiss, no matter if a prince delivers it or a wolf.

My hands on her hips, I lift my head a little from the ground, ever so slowly nearing her. The next moment, Riley pushes back her hood to her shoulders with both hands. Her wild hair frames her face, a few locks tangling across her forehead. The happy gleam in her eyes changes abruptly when she looks into mine. Suspicion crumples her face. "Jack! Were you just going to kiss me?"

Okay, that was a fail.

Motionless from astonishment, I quirk my brows. "Maybe…?"

Now would be a good time for her to get off me. But she doesn't. Her face is still only inches from mine, and she's obviously looking for some sanity in my expression. "Why would you do that?"

My head drops back to the ground. Cumbersome

under her weight, I shrug my shoulders.

Her expression turns grim. "Well, stop it. How would that look if my future husband saw me kissing a stranger?"

My eyes fly wide open. "A stranger?" Hell, I've known this girl for centuries! I lift her off me, then stand up and help her to her feet, maybe pulling a little too hard because she knocks into my chest. I glare down at her face. "What am I to you? Stage equipment?"

Instantly, her expression softens. "Ah, come on, Jack. You know what I mean."

No, actually, I don't.

She must be reading my nonplussed look correctly because she makes a tiny pout and continues. "You're the bad Wolf, eating my family. Obviously, you can't be my happily ever after. But I want one. Not just one kiss. A complete ending—"

"With a prince and all..." I finish for her, rolling my eyes.

Riley takes a wary step back, studying me with narrowed eyes. "Why are you so touchy all of a sudden?"

I pick up her strewn arrows and hold them out to her, growling, "Because your royal gibberish is crap."

Her chin dips down.

"I don't want you to drop out of our story. Maybe it's not the best one ever, but it's good the way it is."

"No, it's not!" she counters, back to boiling with anger as she stuffs the arrows into the quiver. "It's not a love story. It can never be because love only happens among certain society circles. Which, sadly, neither of us belongs to."

"Is that really what you think?"

"History proves it."

"Fine. Then go shoot Arthur with Cupid's arrow." I wave an arm toward Camelot. "Find your gooey ending. I'm out." Spinning on my heels, I trudge back in the direction we came from.

Behind me, it's silent. Riley is probably just standing still, not going anywhere. Otherwise, I would hear her footsteps. Whatever. She can grow roots and hook up with a tree for all I care.

"Jack, wait!" her voice drifts to me a few seconds later. I don't stop, so she runs after me and slows down at my side. I don't spare her a glance. Cautiously, she touches my elbow. "I don't want you to be mad at me."

That ship has sailed.

"What's the problem with it?" When I'm still silent, not slowing down at all, she slips in front of me and forces me to a halt with her palms on my chest. "Please, talk to me."

My sinister scowl doesn't make her move out of my way, so eventually, I give in and growl, "How would you feel if I told you out of the clear blue sky that I wanted to replace you in our story? That I wanted to find a"—I roll my eyes—"suitable mate, with no thought about *your* future? As the girl from the woods, I guess you could play Dracula's bait."

"Is that it?" Her expression turns so soft and pitiful it's disgusting. "Are you scared of what will happen to you once I change my ever after?"

I push her out of the way none too gently and forge on. She's back at my side in an instant, but this time, she walks with me in complete silence for a long time. When we reach the signpost at our usual meeting place, she stops. I can feel her sad gaze following me as I walk on. Her stare is boring into my back like a glowing lance.

Slowing down, I tilt my head back to sigh at the sky and shove my hands into my pockets before I turn around. A flicker of hope—a very little one—crosses her honey eyes. We stare at each other for like half a minute. Eventually, she takes a few reluctant steps toward me.

"You know, we could find you a happy ending, too, if you want." Her suggestion surprises me. And it's not at all what I want. A foot away from me, she stops and cocks her head with a weak smile. "Unfortunately, you broke the other love arrow, or we could have used it on the Queen of Hearts for you."

In spite of my anger, she raises a small smile from me with that. It fades again quickly, though, and I push out a long breath. "I don't want no queen."

All I want is a girl with a red cloak. In what way I want her…I don't actually know at the moment.

"Take care, Riley." I slip my hand between her hair and her neck to pull her closer and place a gentle kiss on her forehead. Then I turn around and leave.

Chapter 5

Riley

Sleep evaded me for most of the night while the spirit of the story tugged at me. I didn't realize it would be so hard to ignore. My thoughts were constantly circling around things I should be doing with Jack in the story. With Granny, too. At some point in the night, I started to wonder if it might be best to drop my idea of finding love, bake a new cake, and just run to my grandmother's house to put everything right.

But I can't. We've come too far to turn back. The day spent with Jack yesterday was so amazingly different. It was funny, it was annoying, it was exciting, and in the end, it was even a little sad. Should it all have been for nothing?

No. I refuse to give up. Somewhere out there is a special happy ending waiting for me, and I'm going to find it. With or without Jack's approval and help. And once I'm set up with my own Prince Charming—or King Arthur— we'll look for *a suitable mate* for Jack, too.

After I finish up my usual morning hot chocolate, I get ready to go to the market. I take the bow and Cupid's arrow with me because I don't intend to return home after meeting up with Cindy. Yesterday, I didn't feel like walking back to Camelot after my fight with Jack. But there's still a king to shoot in the heart.

The market in Grimmwich always bustles with people on Mondays. Stands filled with fruits and veggies line the cobblestone streets around the majestic fountain in the middle of the place. Francois, the baker, tosses me a warm croissant as I pass him. He always does. It's his way of saying thanks for the turkeys I shoot for him in the woods before Thanksgiving and Christmas each year. With a smile, I nod at him and pluck off a piece of the pastry with my fingers to pop into my mouth. Mmh, it's so delicious. The only thing that tastes better is vanilla pudding. Actually, vanilla pudding inside the croissant would be amazing.

Reaching the stone fountain with its three brass nymphs in the middle and water pouring from their jugs, I sit down on the edge and wait for my friend. In the crystal-clear pool, a swarm of goldfish lazily glides through the water. When the last crumbs of my second breakfast rain into the pond, they eagerly suck them up with their toilet seat mouths. It's so funny to watch.

"Hi, sweetie."

At Princess Cinderella's voice, I stand up and greet her with a hug. She always looks fantastic, no matter if she's wearing one of her many princess gowns or, like today, skinny jeans and a light-blue tank top. It must be amazing to have such a wide selection of clothes.

The greeting embraces continue on with Aurora because she and her husband, Prince Phillip, notice us from across the street, and Rory pulls him over. "Ladies," he greets us with a smile and a head tilt, his hands tucked into his jeans' pockets. Rory still clings to his arm.

I like Phillip. Of all my friends' husbands, he's the most laid-back. Cindy's Jason always sticks with social etiquette, even outside of their tale, which is annoying because I know *nothing* about royal customs. Belle's beastly Prince Dominic is a little too touchy at times—you always need to be careful about cracking jokes regarding hair in your soup when he's around. And Prince Finnegan can't keep his hands to himself when Snow-White is around. I once heard Phillip teasing him about keeping the fairy tale porn for when they were alone in their bedroom. I almost choked on my tea, but it's true. Having the lovebirds snogging each other beside you is exhausting because, at some point, you just don't know where to look anymore.

Phillip is probably the guy I would most want my own prince to be like. Because he's so wonderfully…normal.

"Have a good time with Jack yesterday?" he asks, his warm look zeroing in on me.

Color shoots to my cheeks. Yikes, did Jack run right off to tell Phillip everything after we parted?

At my surprised expression, Phillip chuckles and adds, "We were together in the pub when he was called to you for the second time. That's rare, isn't it?"

Oh, *that's* what he means. "Yeah, um…"

"What?" Aurora cuts me off. "You had to play twice?" And then she laughs, Cindy joining in. "Doesn't sound like you got a chance for romance then." Because her husband throws her a questioning look at her words, she feels completely entitled to expose me. "Riley's on the hunt for true love these days. She's sick of sticking around barking Jack and having to endure his bites."

Phillip raises an eyebrow at me, quietly asking, "Sick?"

"Well…tired," I meekly correct so it sounds a little less mean. I know he and Jack are best friends. And since my wishes are being discussed in front of an outsider anyway, why not tell them all the real story of yesterday afternoon. I would have told Cindy while shopping later, but now works just as well.

"We didn't actually play out the second tale yesterday," I explain, walking through the market with all of them following. "Things already started out in a crazy way, so I begged Jack to break out with me and help me find a prince."

Cindy's eyes pop wide, and her mouth hangs open. "You did?"

"Mm-hmm."

"And he *came*?" Phillip chuckles, but he looks even more surprised than Cindy and his wife combined.

"Er…not straight away." A little bashful, I concentrate on a box of peaches sitting on a fruit stand, feeling up a couple and then placing them back. "I had to persuade him. Later, he helped me steal a branch from Cupid's tree so I could make an arrow from it."

Cindy gives a vendor two doubloons for a new crystal hairclip and asks over her shoulder, "What for?"

"I'm going to shoot me a prince with it."

"Oh, man," Phillip groans, a half-torn, half-amused look on his face. He lays an arm around Rory's shoulders and pulls her to his side, her pink summer dress making his white shirt shine even more in the warm morning sun. "And Jack is fine with that plan?" he inquires.

"Not exactly," I murmur. "I don't think he likes being replaced in our story by King Arthur."

"King Arthur?" Now, Phillip laughs out loud and rakes a hand through his blond hair. "You don't ever do things by halves, do you, Riley?"

I smile a little. "Not if I can help it."

"So, what are you going to do if the arrow doesn't work?" Aurora gives words to justified reason. Then her face turns grave. "I really hope you're not going to kill Artie with it."

"I don't know. Lay a trail of chocolate leading to my house, maybe?" I shrug. "I haven't thought that far ahead yet."

Her face contemplative, Rory scratches her nose. I love it when she does that because she always comes up with the greatest ideas then. And sure enough, a few seconds later, her expression lights up as she turns to her husband. "You know what? It's your birthday on Friday, right? So how about we cancel our cruise to Treasure Island this weekend and throw a party instead?"

"A party?" His suspicious gaze wanders from his wife to me, then farther on to Princess Cinderella, and back to Aurora.

"Yes. A really big one. We'll invite all our royal friends and relatives. Riley could pick a prince from the crowd, and she won't have to kill him."

While he mulls over her idea, rubbing the stubble on his chin, I burst out, "Me? In a hall full of princes?" That wouldn't help my problem a lot.

"Why not?" Rory demands.

Clasping my red cloak and the worn dress underneath to point out the obvious, I explain, "Because I'm the girl from the woods." That's what Jack called me anyway. "I don't look like royal dating material. If they even notice me, they would probably just ask me to serve them a drink." With a magical arrow and my shooting skills, things could work out. But relying on sheer dumb luck to bump into a prince who'll fall undyingly in love with me? That's beyond fairy tale material.

"If you're going to wear this"—Cindy grabs my cloak and throws me a wry glance—"they just might. But if you come in a beautiful gown and do your hair for once, you'll look like a real princess."

"Gown or not, most people around here know me." I fold my arms. "They'll recognize me with the first glance."

"We could make it a masked ball," Aurora offers. "Everyone wearing those beautiful face masks. You'd be safe." She beams at her husband. "Wouldn't it be great if Riley married into the family?"

Cindy claps her hands in elation, and finally, I think this new idea actually has some potential. I do own a very pretty dress from my mother. This might be the perfect occasion to get it out of the chest.

"You chicks are crazy," Phillip says, laughing. Then he plants a kiss on Rory's temple. "But if that's what you want, sweetness, we'll have a masked ball for your friend."

She closes her eyes for the length of the kiss and then grins at me brightly, obviously satisfied.

Phillip releases her and gives us all a charming smile. "If you'll excuse me now. I should go talk to someone and investigate the level of his depression after hearing this news." He says the last in a joking manner, but there's a small glint of sincerity in his eyes when his gaze lingers on me for another moment. Hopefully, he can cheer Jack up.

The girls and I stroll off, marveling at the many

beautiful items the vendors present on their stands. Rory and Cindy buy some more stuff, while they squeeze all the details of yesterday out of me. When I get to the part where Jack caught me in his arms, and we fell to the ground, me on top of him, my cheeks warm a little, and I lower my gaze. "I think he was going to kiss me."

"Whoo-hoo!" both my friends holler, high-fiving each other, and I quickly dash an uncomfortable glance around, hoping that no one got big ears at that. Pinocchio winks at me as he passes us, but he seems to be the only one who noticed the girls' outburst of enthusiasm.

"Shhh!" I shut them down. "This isn't funny. And he shouldn't be doing it just because he's scared to lose our boring story. He'll just ruin my chances of getting a prince."

"Forget the prince and stick with the sexy Wolf," Aurora mocks me, but she understands my problem and sobers quickly.

Cindy loops her arm through mine and explains in a soft, patronizing voice, "Don't worry, Riley. If you'd kissed him, no prince would hold that against you. It's not like you gave your virginity to him with a simple kiss."

"No, but my first kiss should be with my one true love," I reason. "I want everything to be perfect."

Rory blows a bubble with the gum she put into her mouth before. After it bursts, she snickers. "Yeah, it would be like a bad joke if, after all these years of being glued to Jack, he was the one snatching the big first."

After talking so much about Jack, and from Phillip's words earlier, I start wondering how Jack is really feeling today. Apart from the constant pull of our story, I mean, because that one I can describe pretty well myself. It's uncomfortable, if not torturous. The hope that some distraction with my friends might ease the nagging sensation has waned by now.

The thought of losing our tale seemed to seriously trouble Jack yesterday. If only he could look at this project with the same enthusiasm I feel. Actually, he should be happy I'm doing the trial run. Because if I fail, nothing bad will happen to him. But if I'm lucky, we can start a second run to set him up with his true love, too.

Gah, boys! Always so blind to awesome new possibilities!

Princess Cinderella, Aurora and I stop for a cappuccino in Remy's bistro and, sitting at a small, round table outside, we make plans for Phillip's birthday party. Of course, I still plan to hunt down Arthur later, but in case I haven't found true love before the weekend, the ball will come in handy.

We just finished, and Cindy is paying for us all—which is very nice of her—when a giant bird lands only a couple of feet away from me. The one-and-a-half-meter wingspan of the stork causes quite the gust, and the wind blows the napkins and bills off several tables around us. Startled, I duck my head until Rory touches my elbow and says, "Oh, look! You got an SMS."

When the wind settles with the bird's wings, I look up in wonder. "What the heck is an SMS?"

"Short Message Stork," she informs me, waving an arm at the black-and-white bird with its long beak. "Have you never gotten one? They're everywhere these days." She rolls her eyes and laughs. "You really are the girl from the woods, aren't you?"

I let that comment pass and warily peek at the feathered avian. "And what is it for?"

"Miss Riley Redcoat?" the stork suddenly speaks up and comes a step closer, its long legs stiff like sticks.

Ugh. "Yes?"

The stork guy salutes me with his wing and continues. "I have a message for you from Granny Redcoat." He clears his throat and suddenly speaks with a completely different voice. One I know too well. "Riley, darling, where are you? I've been waiting for your visit since yesterday. Shouldn't you be stopping by with cake and wine? The Wolf wasn't here, either. I hope he didn't get you in trouble." A shiver trails down my back. It sounds as if my grandmother is standing right in front of me. The stork looks me sternly in the eyes and speaks on in Granny's voice. "I'll wait two hours. If I don't hear from you, I'll file a missing person's report." And then the stork's huge eyes soften. "Love you. Granny."

"Wicked." I'm still staring at the bird with an open mouth. When he keeps looking at me intently, I chip out a formal yet hoarse, "Thank you."

The stork spreads his wings, ready to take off, but Aurora is faster and grabs him by one wing to hold him down, startling not only him but also me. "Don't you want to send your gran a message back?" she asks me, her gaze incredulous.

"Oh. Is that possible?"

"You bet, silly. Just tell him where to deliver it and then dictate the message."

"Okay. Then…um…" I cough slightly and turn back to the stork with a straight spine, speaking out loud and clear. "This is a reply for Granny Redcoat." After that, I hesitate a moment. Damn, what do I even say?

Because the stork starts to look a little impatient, I quickly mumble, "Granny. Something came up, but I'm fine. You don't need to worry. Jack is well, too. I'll come by later this week to explain everything." Okay, that didn't sound too bad. Cindy and Rory fix me with expectant stares, so I add, "I love you, too. Riley."

Proud, I nod at the SMS so he knows that I'm done. In the next second, he takes off, ruffling the updo of Madame Goat, who's walking by with her seven young kids, the smallest of them sitting in a stroller that she pushes down the street.

"Boy, that was crazy," I say with fervor when my friends still watch me as if *I* was the odd thing in the whole situation. "Who's inventing such amazing stuff?"

"The Evil Queen recently expanded her apple production and delivery service, *E*-Apple," Cindy explains.

"From what Snowy said, she was always more into technology than poison."

Snow-White's stepmother is behind this? How cool is that? "So, how do these storks operate? Do I have to buy one to use it?"

"No, sweetie, they're free for all." She points up, and I lift my gaze. A few single storks cross the sky. "The stork net is still thin, but *E*-Apple is working to cover the whole country soon. If you have a message for someone, you only need to lift your hand and do this." Cindy taps her middle finger and thumb together twice. "One of them will come down then and take up your message."

"That is so crazy!"

"No. Crazy is that even your granny knows how to send an SMS and you don't." Giggling, Rory gently pokes me with her elbow as we stand up and leave the café. "Maybe it really *is* time for you to come out of the forest and move into a proper castle. Your new prince can show you all the glorious things that you've missed."

Which totally reminds me of my date with King Arthur. "You're right. I better get going and give this arrow a test drive." I confidently pat the string of my bow across my chest.

Cindy scrunches her face. "Don't hurt him."

We hug and say goodbye, then Aurora laughs, tugging playfully at my hair. "Send us an SMS later and tell us how it went."

I grin and nod because I'd love to use another stork

today. We head in opposite directions, my way getting me out of Grimmwich and through the forest once more. Coming to the signpost and not finding Jack waiting there for me feels strange. But, frankly, so have the past twenty-four hours. I better get used to this feeling soon if I don't want it to distract me from my plan.

Except, that's easier said than done. Of course, it's nothing personal and only has to do with the pull of the story. But the deeper I walk into the woods, the more I miss Jack. If yesterday afternoon proved one thing, it was that it's more fun to go on a mission with him than alone. By the time Cupid's giant tree comes into view in the middle of the lush green clearing, the stupid longing has me wound so tightly in a knot that I'm seriously considering turning around and going to visit Jack instead. He mentioned renting an apartment above Geppetto's workshop. Can't be too hard to find, right?

Then a different idea takes shape. One that sparks a tiny grin. I lift my arm high above my head and tap my middle finger and thumb together a couple of times. Moments later, the flapping of a stork's mighty wings in front of me makes me back up two steps.

"Hello, Mr. Stork," I say warily as he stalks toward me with expectant eyes and taps against a nametag attached to his blue vest. "Oh. Reginald," I correct politely.

He waits. My eyes dart anxiously around the place. "Miss?" he prompts me.

"Oh, yes, sure." I clear my throat vigorously and then

say loud and clear again, like earlier at Remy's, "This is a message for Jack Wolf." Suddenly, I remember that he might not know where Jack lives. But if I ask that now, will he report it in the message? Sheesh! A little panicky, I clasp his beak shut with both hands and send him a pleading look. "Do you even know where to find him?"

"Mmwwmm," he murmurs and flaps his wing against my hands until I let his beak go again. "Madam, do you mind?!" Indignant, he straightens his vest and flexes his beak at the same time. "Storks have a photographic memory, and *E*-Apple constantly provides us with updates about the country and its recipients. I will recognize the bad Wolf when I see him."

"Okay, sure. Sorry. Um, yeah…" My face shrinks to a helpless raisin. "Let's continue then, shall we?"

He gives a formal nod to my incomprehensible stammering.

"Hello, Jack, this is Riley. I was"—*worried about you? Missing you? Freaking out because I don't know what to do outside the story all by myself?*—"wondering what you're doing. Yesterday was such a crazy day. Everything about it." I pause, but only briefly. The stork shouldn't think I'm done. "Anyway, I hope we're still friends. And if we are, I would love to…er…find my romance with you. No, no!" Hysterically, I wave my hands at the SMS as if that will make Jack understand my message any better. "Not *together* with you. Just… Well, it would be nice if you came on this adventure with me." I sigh and instantly wonder if the sound will be delivered in the message, too. "Alone is boring. So, if you don't have any other plans for today, maybe you want to come to Camelot. I guess I'll be hanging out there and stalking the king for a while."

Okay. That was a good message. Well done, Riley. So what are the right words to close this SMS because "*I love you, too*," like I used with my granny is certainly the wrong way to go. Thoughtfully, I narrow my eyes at the stork, but my expression lights up when I remember the many letters I wrote to the *Magical Press*, complaining about the missing deliveries of *The Character Magazine*. With a strong voice I finish, "Sincerely yours, R dot Redcoat."

The stork rolls his eyes. Totally back to feeling insecure with this whole message delivery thing, I ask him, "Not good?"

"Perfect," he replies with dry sarcasm and beats his wings to fly off.

Craning my neck, I watch him disappear into the clouds. He's long gone when I finally turn back to the path in front of me and make my way through the Plush Toy Forest and across Kansas toward Camelot. Every now and then, my glance travels up to the sky, hoping that Jack might send a reply with a stork. Apart from Nils Holgersson traveling south with his wild geese, there's nothing to report.

Well, lighten up, Riley. You can do this alone, as well.

Only, I didn't lie earlier. Alone isn't half as much fun as together. I wish Jack had come. My shoulders are hanging depressively, as are the corners of my mouth, by the time I slip into the bushes close to King Arthur's castle.

I wait a few minutes, ducking in the shrubs as if on a turkey hunt. This is a good hiding place. There are no guards anywhere near. Breaking into the castle and confronting Arthur with the arrow pointing at him surely isn't the best way to go about things. Better wait until he comes out into his fine garden. He can't hide inside forever, right? Even though after an hour and a half, it certainly looks like it.

Man, doesn't he need fresh air?

Just when I'm starting to believe that my adventure will be delayed again, the mighty wooden door of the castle opens. A young man in a white shirt and leather pants with a beard and a crown sitting askew on his head appears in the warm afternoon light.

My heart starts to pound dramatically in my chest. This is it. The moment when I'll change my fate. Boy, am I nervous all of a sudden. My clammy fingers can hardly draw the bow with Cupid's arrow as I stand up and watch King Arthur from behind a cherry tree. He bends down and plucks a few tulips from the majestic flowerbed near his feet. Good. He can give them to me in a minute when my arrow nails him in the heart, and he falls head over heels in love with me.

The sinew of the bow sounds out with tension as I draw the string even tighter. An excited smile pulls hard at my mouth.

"Well, hello there, Miss Redcoat… Found your target, I see."

Nearly jumping out of my skin, I whirl around to the voice behind me and point the arrow's tip straight at Jack's chest.

Chapter 6

Jack

Once again, I find myself in the line of fire. This time, instead of pushing the arrow away, I only lift my hands in surrender and smile at Riley.

"Jack!" She eases off the string and lowers the bow. "You came!" The joy in her voice and eyes is sincere. I didn't expect anything less. From her whimsical message earlier, I figured she wanted me here.

Still, it didn't make me come any faster. I drop my hands and tuck them into my pockets. Frankly, finding a stork at my window after Phillip left was quite the surprise.

Her message made me laugh, though. And it made me sad at the same time. For a solid hour, I paced my apartment, trying to make a decision. Erase Riley from my life completely, or start something entirely different with her?

A friendship outside of our tale.

I think that's what she was asking me for in her SMS anyway—if we could have this tiny thing between us, even though we stopped playing our story every day.

Last night was tough. I've never had to fight against the call of the forest before. This must be what it feels like to break an addiction. There was a point sometime after midnight when I cursed Riley for doing this to me. But a life totally without her after being bound to her from the onset of fairy tales? It was hard to imagine.

Well, I'm here now, so I guess my decision is clear.

A sigh wants out of my throat, but I force it down. "I can't let my girl shoot somebody without me, can I?"

She laughs. "Your girl?"

"You've been that for centuries, yes," I answer sentimentally. But then I let a smirk take up residence on my face to ease the annoying lump in my throat. "And I believe it entitles me to co-determine the right happily ever after for you."

Riley takes a step back and leans against the tree, bow and arrow crossed in front of her thighs. The red cloak accentuates the mischievous spark in her honey-colored eyes. "Oh, you want voting rights in my choice?"

"That's what I'm saying." Cocking my head, I tilt my

eyebrows once. "And that guy"—I nod toward Arthur in his garden a couple of hundred feet away from us, totally unaware what kind of fate awaits him—"isn't the right one for you."

"Thanks. Your concern is duly noted." She sticks out her tongue at me, which makes me want to teach her another lesson. But she turns away from me, laughing, and draws the bow again, pointed in the same position as before. "Too bad there're only two of us. And if it's a tie, it's my choice that counts since it's my H.E.A. we're voting on."

"H.E.A?"

"Happily ever after," she explains gossip girl talk to me. Then she utters a curse under her breath.

"What is it?" I whisper, coming to her side to have a closer look at the palace garden. King Arthur isn't alone anymore. Some of his knights, among them Sir Lancelot, gather around him. That's a problem for her, indeed.

"Tough luck. Looks like they're starting a new play." I don't know why I'm grinning now. Okay, that's a lie. I do know why. "This can go on for days, you know. And you can't shoot Arthur out of his tale."

"That's what you think?" Her question sounds very much like a dare. Bow drawn right beside her jaw, one eye closed, the other narrowed for aim, she pulls at the string so hard that the wood bends. The sound gives me chills of the uncomfortable kind.

Riley is an excellent archer. She can shoot a cherry off

a tree from three hundred feet away. Six feet of king flesh a short distance from us isn't a challenge. If I let her fire this arrow now, though, I'll lose her. I'll lose our tale and my job. Damnit, she'll turn my whole life upside down with one shot.

Panic rises inside me, hot like the coals in her granny's stove. I can't let her do this. Not so fast. Not today!

Short of a better idea, I lean in to her ear just when she's ready to let go and drawl, "They say Guinevere ran off because he stinks like a polecat."

Her eyes jerk open, and she stiffens in shock, but the arrow is gone. Holding my breath in terror, I whip around and track its path. It's a short miss on Arthur, the arrow zooming past his face, embedding in the tree behind him. The thud echoes loudly, the sound carrying over to us.

Riley and I stand rigidly in the bushes, staring at Arthur like ghosts shut out from a haunted castle. Tracing the direction where the arrow came from, he swings around. I don't know who's more shocked, him or us. But he sure gets out of his stupor quicker than we do. Arm stretched out, a finger pointing at our hideout, he yells at those who swore him fealty, "Invaaadors!"

Next thing I know, a hoard of knights in tinny armor raise their swords and comes barreling toward us. My heart kicks into gear. Because Riley still stares at the lost arrow, paralyzed, I grab her hand and drag her with me. *"Run!"*

It takes half a second before she switches into flight mode, and I don't have to pull so hard on her hand anymore. As we jump over the underbrush, she straps the bow to her back. The weapon out of the way, she finally moves faster, and we have a chance of escaping our pursuers. But with my supersensitive hearing, I realize there's a whole new problem behind us. Hoofbeats. King Arthur sent his mounted henchmen after us, and *they* will catch us in less than a minute.

Great! Just what I wished for when I decided to seek out Red Riding Hood here. Becoming a target myself.

Riley runs fast, but her legs are a lot shorter than mine. I could be out of here in three seconds. She can't.

"Get on my back!" I shout as we reach the beaten track.

"What?"

"Don't question! Just do it!" I let go of her hand and will the Wolf inside me to the surface. Falling from a two-legged sprint into a four-legged one without missing a beat, I sidle up closer to Riley. A little screech escapes her, but at my nudging on her hip with my flank, she finally catches on. Her frightened hands clasp my fur. Two more steps and she throws herself on top of me, slinging her arms around my neck. I give her another second to straddle my back, then I really accelerate, pounding my paws on the dirt.

Because she keeps me in a terrified chokehold, I'm confident that she won't get lost if we go cross-country. It's the only chance we have to outdistance the galloping army closing in on my haunches. As we slip through the bushes and jump over some fallen wood, Riley whimpers in my ear. "By Grimm's undying soul! Jack, you will kill us."

No, her lovely King Arthur will kill us. And it's all her fault. I refuse to be the impressive wolf hide hung on the wall in his cold throne room tonight.

With a good lead on the horsemen, I keep an eye out for a hiding place and skitter to a halt when I spot something like a fox's den or a badger's burrow in the roots of a giant cypress tree.

"Why did you stop?" Riley hisses, and it feels like she's anxiously turning around to look out for our followers.

Because I can't speak as a wolf, I shake her off my back. With a protesting *humph*, she lands in the moss. Sniffing the den for residents, I find nothing. There's no animal in it—probably hasn't been for several weeks. I hustle Riley toward the entrance, and when she's finally crouching in front, I push her inside with my snout. Fortunately, the den is big enough for both of us. I crawl in after her, careful that my tail doesn't stick out when the hooves of the kingmen's horses tromp past outside.

We huddle together in the darkness and stare out. Riley is shaking like a leaf. Her erratic breaths puff into my ear, which is quite uncomfortable because, so close, it has the power of a wind gust. My ear twitches uncontrollably at each blast.

Well, I'm sure she didn't imagine that her first encounter with her adorable king would end in a deadly hunt.

After a couple of minutes, the sound of galloping fades away, and no more knights seem to follow. *Phew.* That was close.

"Do you think they're gone?" Riley hisses in my ear.

I wasn't prepared for that. With a tortured yip, I cringe away. Riley jerks, too. And suddenly, her shriek breaks through the den behind me. The little light coming from the entrance is just enough to highlight that she's falling—or about to.

Zooming after her, I only catch her cloak with my teeth. I have to dig all four paws into the ground to keep from being pulled after her as she dangles in the air. Crap, I have no idea where I maneuvered us but, apparently, this is not a badger's nest. In the darkness behind us is an abyss, and Riley is hanging over the edge with only my hold on the red fabric keeping her from plummeting to her death.

"Jack! Get me out of here!" she cries in sheer panic, her weight dragging me closer to the edge. I get a glimpse down and, holy twisted hat of the Mad Hatter, the hole must be sixty feet deep. There's a little coffee table with a peacefully burning candle casting a faint light at the bottom of the abyss. The black-and-white-checkered floor spans the length and width of a tiny, square room with one small door on the left.

Awesome! I guess we found the rabbit's hole.

"Jaaack! *Please*!" The shriek assaults my ears. Instinctively, I flatten them.

Oh, right. Red Riding Hood! I start pulling at her

cloak until she comes back over the edge. A relieved breath wheezes out of her lungs once she's safely back on the ground. We should really get out of here. The entrance to Wonderland is not a place to toy with. I lower my muzzle and whine, giving Riley a push with my forehead.

She nods, understanding my hint. On her hands and knees, she crawls out of the den first. Because there's next to no room in the burrow to move, my snout presses to her skirt-covered bottom. In wolf form? That's asking for trouble.

As the sweet scent of innocence drifts to my nostrils, my head gets a little woozy. Weird thoughts spring to my mind. I salivate. If there weren't a dress and her cloak between us, I would probably be lashing out now and stealing a taste of the forbidden apple.

I can barely shake off the urge when Riley disappears from the exit, and sunlight blinds me. For a brief second, I can't see anything. Heck, where did she go? I need to breathe that fragrance in again. It's so delicious.

Shaking my head once, I find her standing a couple of feet away from the tree, patting dirt off her cloak. *Don't bother, babe, I like it dirty.* I can do nothing about the low growl that rumbles from my throat as I prowl closer to my prey. Heat sizzles through my entire body, raising my hackles and putting all my senses on high-alert. Damn, I need to screw or eat someone. Preferably both, in that particular order.

Riley's wary gaze finds me and lingers. Right, that's

the perfect mix. Innocence and a dash of fright. She couldn't tease me any more than this if she tried.

"Jack? Is everything all right?"

It will be, honeydrop, when you bend over for me.

"Could you please stop that?" Her hands flash out defensively, and she stumbles back a few steps until she hits a tree. "You're scaring me."

I'm not going to hurt you. My eyes turn to slits as I sneer. *Well, not very much.*

Body and hands flattened against the trunk behind her, she's trapped. Nice. A luxurious snarl escapes from between my teeth. I'm really hungry.

"Okay, listen! This is *not* funny!" The anger in her voice doesn't override the fear in her eyes. And it sure won't make me stop. She denied me a decent granny dinner yesterday, so I guess it's only fair that I swallow Red Riding Hood now instead. She looks much more tender than the old lady anyway. I bet she tastes devilishly good.

Taller than the average wolf, my eyes are at the level of her perfect, apple-shaped breasts when I reach her. Her chest lifts and falls with her anxious breathing. A titillating sight, and a good place to sink my teeth in, but there's something else drawing me in harder.

I dip my head low and search out the wonderful scent of the sweet innocence between her legs again. Shish kebob or shag? What do I go for? My mouth waters. Would she scream if I tore her clothes off with my teeth right here against the tree?

"Good *Grimm*! Are you sniffing me?!"

Her outraged voice echoes around us, but I don't hear what she's saying anymore. This other part of her speaks to me much louder and clearer. All right, so the shag it is. The thick fur at my neck rises in anticipation. Finally, I have this girl exactly where I've always wanted her. At my mercy. And from the tearing hunger still boiling in my veins, cooking my blood, I can no longer promise that I'll have any patience with her. She's mine. To take. To play with. And to eat when I'm done with her.

Except, Riley tugs her cloak closed in front of my muzzle as if she's shutting a door. "Lay off, you pervert! I'm not a dog!" And then a sharp twinge shoots from my nose up to my eyes as she boxes me on the snout.

Yipping in pain, I back down, crossing my front paws over my muzzle on the forest floor. Tears spring to my eyes. I actually forgot how much this hurts. Like someone's doing a root canal without anesthetic. The smack was enough to clear the haze from my mind. I'm back in control but, hell, that was close.

As the pain eases, I lift my head to look at Riley. She's still pressing against the tree, and the fright is quite apparent in her eyes. Only now, she's holding her bow, arrow aimed at me.

To give her the proof of safety, I change back to the man I am ninety percent of my life. Slowly coming to my feet, I don't let her gaze escape mine. She's good at trailing tracks. The apology in my eyes shouldn't be hard for her to read. "I'm sorry. You can lower the bow now. I won't hurt you."

A weak, almost hysteric, and very, very insecure "huh" escapes her.

I step up to her and carefully lower her weapon. "Promise."

After some resistance, she relents with a deep sigh. But then she runs a hand through her wild hair. "Holy land of plenty, Jack! What got into you?"

There's no use lying to her now. That was a close call, and with her stupid idea of going on tale strike, she's not only casting a painful spell of abstinence on me but also putting herself in deadly danger.

"Instincts took over. It's a damn struggle, and it hurts. I don't know how much longer I can withstand the call of the woods. Or the story." When she tucked the arrow back into her quiver, I take her hand, pleading with her. "Don't you feel it, too?"

Her eyes widen in shock, but not from fear like before. I think there might be sympathy shining in them now. "Well, yeah. Probably. It feels weird. Like someone's constantly trying to meddle with my mind and make me go in another direction than what I want. But I guess it's harder for you than for me because you also have to fight against the Wolf inside you." Her gaze turns a notch softer. "I'm sorry, Jack. I didn't mean to hurt you with all this. But I can't just turn back now. Can you understand that?"

Yes, I can. It doesn't mean I have to like it. And since

we're obviously going on with this odd adventure, we need to take some precautions—put rules in place—for her safety. Because it won't be long before the Wolf comes out again. And the next time, I'm pretty sure he'll choose food over the shag. I tug at her hand and head off along the path leading back to her house in Glitter Hollow.

My strides are fast, and she's falling in and out of a jog to keep up with me. "Where are you taking me?" she demands, panting.

"Home."

"Why? I haven't caught me a prince yet."

"Your love arrow is lost, and it's getting late," I growl. "You can go on a prince hunt again tomorrow."

I don't know if it's my commanding voice that shuts her up, or the sympathy she still holds for me because of what I told her earlier. Whichever, I'm just glad we don't have to start a discussion over it now.

A little while later, her hut appears in front of us. Pulling Riley up the steps of the small porch, I open the door and then push her inside.

She whirls around to me with worry in her eyes. "What's going on?"

Sweat is beading on my forehead. Shit. I was hoping I could hold the Wolf back for a little while longer, but it's rebelling inside me so hard that I'm actually thinking about eating Riley in the form I'm in right now.

Get a grip, Jack!

Squeezing my eyes shut, I shake my head once. Then I

turn back to her with stern insistence in my gaze. "Lock the door and all the windows. And if I come to you tonight, you better not open."

Her lovely lips part with shock. Good. Finally, she understands the gravity of her decisions. I force my hand to remain steady as I gently stroke my knuckles over her pale cheek. "Riley?" I rasp, demanding her acknowledgement.

Reluctantly, she nods, giving me her promise. Releasing an actually painful breath, I turn around and trudge down the steps, walking away.

"Jack?"

At her quiet voice, I stop but don't turn around, only grumble, "Mm?" with my hard gaze on the dark forest in front of me.

The sound of her soft footsteps on the wooden planks drifts from the porch. "Will you be all right?"

Without giving her an answer, I leave.

Hopefully, the girl does what she's been told for once. Since I have no idea what my Wolf will do if freed in this agitated state, I better not take any chances with her. She's so breakable and innocent. In her naivety, a simple lie might be enough for her to let me in. And that will probably be the end of Red Riding Hood altogether.

I don't want to hurt Riley. Desperately running my hands through my hair, a deep growl erupts from me. Fuck. It already begins. In this unpredictable state, I can't return to my own apartment. A locked bedroom door won't keep me trapped for long.

The forest hazes through my vision as I take a turn to Castle Grove and forge on through the clutter of trees and bushes, stumbling from one side to the other, sometimes catching hold of the rough bark of a tree trunk, other times just falling to my knees. It takes an immeasurable amount of willpower to fight against the Wolf on the rise. He can't come out yet.

Rubbing the sweat from my face, I try to figure out where I am. The pink tips of a castle loom behind the crowns of a line of ash trees. Thank Grimm, it's not so far anymore.

As I fight forward, my breathing becomes increasingly labored until I cross a stone bridge over a moat and finally fall against a heavy wooden door. With a weak fist, I hammer against it as hard as my waning strength allows.

Even though it's probably only seconds, it feels like hours until someone opens up. A shooting star of relief zaps through me as I look into the shocked blue eyes of the only person in Fairyland I trust my life to.

Grabbing the doorframe for support, I pant, "Phil! You need to help me!"

Chapter 7

With Jack's warning still ringing in my ears hours later, I huddle behind the couch and point Uncle Elmer's old shotgun at the door, too scared to even blink. The only company I have through the lonely night is the annoying tick-tock of the grandfather clock by the wall. Sometimes, I wonder if it wants to deliberately lure me to sleep so the big, bad Wolf can come into my house and eat me.

But Jack doesn't return. In the early morning hours, and after three visits from the sandman, I finally lose the fight and let my eyes drift shut, my finger still on the trigger…

A pack of ravenous wolves chases me through the forest in my dreams, a handsome prince waiting and waving at me ahead. But no matter how fast I run toward him, he continues to hover just beyond my reach.

As a sharp knock on wood echoes, the prince and I both jerk our heads. The gun in my hand fires—

My eyes pop open at the thunderous bang, and I find that, luckily, the bullet went through the ceiling and not the door.

Panic grabs me for a moment at the thought that Jack has finally come for me. "Who is it?" I call out, wiping drool off the corner of my mouth as I straighten from the couch and walk to the door, the gun at the ready.

Alarmed not by my voice but more than likely by the shot, someone outside shouts back, "Riley, are you okay?"

Thank the thirteen fairies it isn't Jack. I lower the rusty, old weapon and rush forward to open the door. "Phillip! Sorry, I didn't mean to shoot at you. I…fell asleep…" My face crumples. "With the gun." Okay, even to me that sounds odd.

Quietly, his guarded gaze drops to the smoke steaming from the barrel of my shotgun before it slowly wanders back up to my eyes. "I see you took Jack's warning seriously."

He knows what Jack said to me before he left? Then again, it's not a big surprise. They must have met afterward. Leaning the gun against the wall next to the door, I step aside and ask my visitor in, confessing, "I think he's a bit out of his mind since we stopped playing."

"Oh, he sure is." Phillip comes through the door and takes a curious look around my small but cozy home. He's never been here before, which hikes up my next suspicion.

"To what do I owe the honor?" I drawl, sweeping my hand toward the couch, offering him a seat. "Did Rory send you?"

Tearing his attention away from my whimsical furniture, his focus sharpens on me once more as his hands disappear into the pockets of his dark leather pants, pushing the red, button-down shirt and white royal vest slightly upward. "Nobody sent me. But I need you to come with me, Riley." Besides the urgency in his tone, I notice that he ignores my offer to sit down and lingers close to the door, which is still open.

My backside pressed against the kitchen table, I grab the wooden edges beside my hips. Lines furrow my brow. "Come with you *where*?"

"To Jack." He takes a step toward me, his chin dipping just a little as he stares down at my face. "He's in trouble, and I believe you're the only one who can help him."

"What?" The tiny word escapes me on a squeak of shock. My fingers loosen from the edge of the table, and I clasp my suddenly clammy hands in front of my stomach. "Where is he? Is anybody hurt? Did Jack eat someone?" Holy honeypot, if he lost control in the village, it's all my fault. I forced this fate on him, even though he told me how hard it was for him to endure. I saw the struggle in his eyes yesterday before he left. "Are the police after him?"

Phillip lays his hands on my shoulders, speaking very softly yet with insistence. "No one got hurt…yet. But it's only a matter of time. Will you please come with me and help me save my friend?"

In a wild panic, I nod and let the prince lead me out of my house. With my brain so fuzzy, I only realize that I'm without my bow and quiver when I pull the door closed. As I turn around to get them, something else grabs my focus.

There's a horse in front of my house.

Phillip walks to the giant white animal, takes the reins, and holds out a hand to me. In response, I lift both of mine in denial. "Nuh-uh!"

"You don't have to be afraid. I'll help you up."

"I've never ridden a horse before," I confess, fear making my voice tremble.

He slips one foot into the stirrup of the lordly black saddle and hoists himself onto the back of the beast. A loud snort puffs out of the horse's nostrils as it shakes its ghostly white mane. When Phillip has a good seat, he gently taps the animal's belly with his heel so it trots toward me.

The gleam in his eyes is a mix of taunt and mischief. "I heard you rode a wolf yesterday," he says, bending down to grab my wrist. In the next moment, I'm lifted up so fast that I can't even protest. "Riding a horse is much the same." He tucks me sideways against his chest and holds me tightly with one arm as he gathers the reins in the other hand and makes the white horse gallop off with an aggressive, "Giddyup!"

My legs dangling over the horse's side, Phillip is the only thing I can hold on to. And I do it with ferocious strength.

"I'm not sure if I've ever seen you scared before, Red Riding Hood," he chuckles into my ear as I press my face against his chest.

I squeeze my eyes shut. "Well, now you know my weakness."

A few minutes later, the sound of hoof beats on the forest floor gives way to the sound of a hard clop on cobblestones. I dare to glimpse at where we are. Expecting a ride through Grimmwich, surprise knocks me dumb because we're crossing the bridge over the moat to Rory's home.

The mighty castle towers over an enchanted circle of thorn hedges around us, and Phillip pulls the horse to an abrupt stop. He gets off first and helps me down with a safe grip on my waist.

By Pinocchio's growing nose, standing on my own feet has never felt so good.

That the magical hedge is still there but lets us ride through it so easily tells me exactly where in their story of *Little Aurora* they are stuck right now. "Is Rory asleep?"

"Yep. Has been for almost a day." A smack on the horse's behind from Phillip is enough to send it trotting away. Apparently, it knows the way to the stables well.

"Why didn't you kiss her?" It should be the first thing for him to do right after breaking through the wild, creeping rose brambles. And why are we here anyway? Didn't he say he was going to take me to Jack?

"Because things will be easier if she sleeps on for a little longer." He opens the door and drags me through.

Everything inside the castle is eerily quiet. The servants are probably napping in the sun. Aurora is supposed to be asleep in a room in the highest tower of the castle, but as we pass the grand stairs leading upward, I realize that's not where we're going.

"I'll kiss her awake soon. But first, we need to solve this problem."

We take a left behind the servants' kitchen, and Phillip picks a burning torch from the wall before he leads me down a set of narrow stone steps. All right, *the problem* must be in the dungeons then. A shiver pleads with me to turn around and run away because damp vaults without any daylight are never a place for a happy story. Phillip seems to sense my worry and wraps his fingers around my hand a little tighter.

"I thought we were going to see Jack? Why are we heading into the dungeon?" I croak in an almost inaudible voice. I don't know why, but dark places always make me whisper.

Phillip pulls me along a narrow corridor, the light from the torch making our shadows perform a spooky welcome dance on the stone walls. He turns his head to me, his gaze serious. "Because Jack is *in* the dungeon. He asked me to lock him away."

His words zap me like Maleficent's evil spell. My mouth tips open, but no sound comes out. Until we round another corner, and I make out the features of a person in a vault behind an iron gate.

My heartbeat clips incredibly fast. Letting go of Phillip's hand, I move closer to the gate, noticing that the young man in there is leaning his head on his forearm, which is braced against the wall. Even though his back is to us, I would recognize him anywhere in the world. "Jack—" I croak.

He's breathing hard, I can see that from here. When he turns his head to look over his shoulder at me, an inhuman sound rumbles from his throat, making me stop in my tracks. His face is covered in sweat. With Phillip's torchlight, I can see that his clothes are also drenched. Wet hair sticks to his forehead, strands of it nearly covering his sinister eyes. "Why did you bring her?" he growls so dangerously my skin rises in goosebumps. Even though I know he's talking to the prince behind me, his gaze bores holes into me.

My hands clapped over my mouth, I try not to tear up as I walk closer to him. "Jack…what hap—?"

In an explosive roar, he leaps away from the wall, changing into the deadly Wolf, and knocks against the gate only inches from my face.

"Baaah!" Terrified, I jump away, bumping into Phillip, who almost drops the torch in surprise. Thankfully, the iron keeps Jack in place, even if his mighty paw claws out through the gaps in the woven metal. His enraged barks and snarls echo through the tunnels.

Phillip steadies me and worriedly searches my face. "Are you all right? He didn't catch you, did he?"

"Ah, yeah…no…I'm fine," I stutter in a whiny voice. Even if he has no trouble ignoring Jack, I can't do that so easily. My torn gaze switches back to the tortured Wolf, and I want to start crying. "What's going on?"

Phillip tucks the torch into an iron claw fastened on the stone wall and puts his hands on my shoulders, gently moving me backward until my legs knock into something hard and I drop sideways onto a wooden chair by the wall. "Jack came to me yesterday. He was in bad shape, asking me for help."

"Help?" I rasp.

"The whole thing with ignoring your tale is getting to him." Phillip lowers into a squat in front of me, holding on to the backrest of the chair. "He knew he couldn't keep the Wolf inside for much longer, so he asked me to lock him down and make sure he didn't wreak havoc. Neither of us knew what to expect, but we both hoped it would ease after a while. It hasn't."

Very slowly, I start taking in the rest of my surroundings. There's a small, round table beside the chair. An open bottle of wine and a used glass on the surface suggest that someone must have been sitting guard here through the night.

"Jack didn't want anyone to know what's happening." Phillip speaks in a calm but firm tone. "I couldn't tell Rory. That's why she's still sleeping. I can't engage in the story as long as my buddy is in trouble." He heaves a sigh. "And he barred me from bringing you here."

"Thanks for coming for me anyway," I whisper. My gaze shifts, and I look over to the still raging Wolf. His animalistic scowl is focused hard on me. It seems he's trying to tear the iron gate apart just so he can get to me. His roar shakes me to the core.

"Don't worry." Phillip interprets my look absolutely right. "He can't get out of there. But we need to do something to help him."

My gaze snaps back to him, and I pant in all sincerity, "Of course. We'll go through with our tale. Well go to Granny and finish what began two days ago. I mean, that should stop his pain and bring him back to normal, right?"

The long silence coming from the prince makes me nervous. "What? You don't think it'll work?"

He sighs. "I'm afraid it's too late for that. He isn't himself anymore. For hours, he's been changing back and forth, uncontrollably. If I open this gate now, he'll descend on me." A short pause. "Right after he eats *you*."

Goodness, I can just see that happening. We'd never make it to Granny's house. If the lunacy in his eyes is anything to go by, we wouldn't even make it around the corner, and Jack would leave a bloody trail in his wake.

"What do you suggest?" I chirp, swallowing hard.

"I have an idea, but it's a long shot." He rises to this feet and starts pacing. The tension in his shoulders reveals that he doesn't put a lot of stock in the plan.

"I guess we don't have much choice right now. So…what is it?"

Blowing out a breath, he turns around to me. "Dr. Jekyll."

A shudder travels down my spine at the name. Dr. Henry Jekyll is a brilliant ENT specialist and pediatrician in town, but I know Phillip isn't speaking about getting sore throat drops for Jack.

The doctor also has a darker side. The scientist in him has been mixing dangerous potions in his laboratory all through his story. His most questionable masterpiece is an elixir originally meant to separate the good side from the evil in a person. In doing so, he ended up creating Mr. Hyde.

Now, I can understand why the idea puts Phillip on edge. "You want him to give Jack some of his mixture. Do you think it'll bring him back?"

"Well, it can't get much worse than this." He gestures toward the Wolf repeatedly running into the gate, the clang echoing through the underground. "It's worth a try. And maybe the only chance we have." He lifts a brow, taunting me in the middle of this already dire situation. "Unless you want to get your bow and release Jack from his torture."

Shoot my friend? "That's not funny," I growl.

Phillip comes closer and hunkers down in front of me again so we're at eye level. "I know." The honesty in his look says that he's just plain overwhelmed and at a loss for what to do next. "I'd really like to get ahold of the doctor, hear what he has to say. Would you stay here and keep an eye on Jack while I ride to town?"

"Of course!" My heart is bleeding for my friend. I'm not going *anywhere* until he's well again.

Phillip nods, standing. "I'll be back as fast as I can."

What I like so much about the prince is that he never hems and haws when it's clearly not the time to. The clip of the heels of his boots echoes and fades as he strides away, disappearing around the corner.

Still shaking from the shock of all of this, I sit rigidly and finally turn my head back to the cell. Jack snarls in the flickering light of the flame. He oozes danger but, for once, he retreats from the gate. We stare at each other for a lengthy moment. By all the rainbows in Fairyland, I wish I could help him.

The snarling ceases. He doesn't bare his teeth at me anymore either. Not letting me out of his sight, he lowers to the cold stone floor in the shadows of his vault. Hope surfaces that he'll soon change back to his human self, realizing that I'm not a piece of meat that Phillip brought here to tease him with.

Breathing in slow and deep, I grasp the backrest of the chair and brace the other hand on the table, pushing myself up. Cautiously, I walk closer to the cage. "Jack? Is that you now?" My voice is nothing more than a mouse squeak in the silent dungeon. "I'm so sorry. You have to know that I never meant to—"

The beast leaps forward once again and crashes headfirst into the gate, making it shudder and sending me back in terror. He falls to the floor, a labored breath puffing out through his snout.

Heartbroken, I press my fists to my mouth and scrunch up my face.

Ouch.

*

Hours must have passed since Phillip left us alone. My back hurts from hunching over the small, round table, peeling the label off the half-empty wine bottle. Merlot. I believe this is a much classier brand than the bottom-shelf liquor I bring to Granny every so often.

Jack became quiet over the last half hour. He stopped maltreating the iron gate to get out and is now lying in the shadowy corner at the back of the vault. Only his eyes sparkle in the dark.

Impatiently, I get up and look around the corner in hopes that the prince might be returning at last. But the cold corridor is still empty. Disheartened, I lower back onto the chair.

"Want to know what I've been wondering all this

time, Jack?" I murmur after some time, concentrating on the final sticky bits of the label. "What Granny does with all the wine I bring to her? I mean, obviously, she can't drink it all or she'd have long since conked out from alcoholic cirrhosis, right? So where does it go? Into a pool behind her house?"

I sniff, rolling the biggest piece of paper I peeled off into a small pellet. "And then I wondered what *you* do outside our tales. The other day when we had to play double was the first time I ever saw you drunk." Okay, he wasn't really drunk, just slightly tipsy, but it made me think about him anyway. About his private life that doesn't include Granny or me. Or even the Huntsman. "We've spent an incredible amount of time together, yet I don't know anything about you or what you like to do. Isn't that odd? I don't know what your favorite food is. If you'd rather sleep in wolf or human form. Or what you wish for when you see a shooting star."

As an extended, dangerous snarl crawls across the stone floor from the farthest corner of the vault, I pull up my feet by instinct as if the sound alone could drag me into the shadows. And then Jack's contemptuous voice flows out of the dark. "I wish I had eaten you that last time at your granny's house."

I stiffen in the chair and snap my head up, my heart beating in my throat. He doesn't come out of the shadows, but his eyes gleam differently now. More brown again than pitch-black.

Three nervous heartbeats pass before my voice returns, and I slowly lift from the chair. "No, you don't mean that, Jack." It's a mere whisper. A plea. I know he's suffering because of my wanton decisions, but he can't hate me that much. Can he? "We're friends."

Rustling on the floor tells me that he's rising. Cautiously, I walk closer, holding my breath, but when he steps out of the darkness into the firelight, my blood curdles, and I freeze.

His chin dipped low, lips compressed into a scathing line, he comes to the gate and scowls at me through a gap in the iron. Thin, bloodied veins spread out in an eerie pattern beneath the skin under his eyes. Sweat drips from his brow, and his nostrils flare as if he can't filter enough air through them to survive.

There, at the corner of his mouth, foam builds and runs down his chin as he drawls in a toxic tone, "That is what *you* think."

Chapter 8

Jack

Riley's eyes mist over in terror. Good. Let's hope that'll finally make her leave. Ever since she stepped foot into these dungeons, her scent has assaulted my nostrils. It's a smell that pulls uncomfortable strings in my head. I want to pierce my fangs into her body and tear her tender flesh from her bones.

But she doesn't run off. Instead, she stays rooted to the ground and murmurs some useless apologies that nobody cares about.

"Open the door!" I snarl, cutting her off, sick of her

bell-like voice, sick of her frightened look, and most of all, sick of her pity. I've been in this vault long enough. I need to run. To hunt. To eat. Where the hell did Phillip go? They were plotting something against me before he left—I heard them, but in my rage to get to the girl, most of what they said was lost.

"Jack…" Her voice trembles. "I can't let you out. It's too—"

"Open this goddamned gate, Red Riding Hood!" I roar, grasping the iron and rattling it so hard, she ducks her head and throws her arms over it in panic. Is that what she does to protect herself? Pathetic. If there wasn't this blasted gate between us, she'd be dead by now. Wolf meal. Bloody hell, I need to get out of here.

"There, there, Jack." Phil's taunting tone rips my gaze away from the girl. "We don't yell at ladies in this castle." Coming around the corner, the bastard smirks as if this was a stupid game we're playing, and he just won because he brought backing.

Who is that guy in the black coat behind him anyway? I think I remember the shaggy, dark hair from somewhere, but I have no name to put to the tall man with the leather bag. His bushy eyebrows tilt, joining together as he examines me from a distance.

"Hello, Doctor Jekyll," the girl greets him, sounding relieved as she shakes his hand. "Thank you for coming."

At the name, something clicks into place in my head, and my grip tightens around the iron. "What the hell did you bring a psychopathic scientist for?" I hiss at Phillip, spitting foam.

"The doctor is here to help you," he replies as he comes forward, his concerned gaze focused on me.

Fuck his worry! I reach through the gaps and claw at his shirt with my fingers. Unfortunately, I don't get ahold of him because the bastard leaps back.

"Oookayyy…" His hands lifted, he turns around to face the girl and the psycho. "You better not get too close, doc."

I stretch my neck, suddenly finding it hard to breathe.

The stranger bends down and opens his black medical bag. Keeping a wary eye on me as he rummages inside the case, he asks Phil, "Are you sure this is just a case of tale denial, and that your friend didn't actually catch rabies somewhere?"

"Come closer, and I'll *give* you rabies," I snarl, rattling the gate once more.

One knee still on the ground, the doctor concentrates on drawing dark green liquid into a syringe.

"What exactly is that?" Red Riding Hood demands, her insecure gaze on the needle.

Yeah, what the hell is that? "Hey! If you turn me into the Hulk, I'll have your heart for breakfast and bury your balls in a hole in the woods. Just so we're clear, psycho."

He throws me a short, demeaning look but talks to the others as he puts the bottle away. "This is a fine-tuned version of my original personality-separating elixir." He flicks his finger twice against the syringe. "It'll isolate the good and the evil parts of your friend. I honed it with pixie dust, thus the glitter in the liquid. It makes sure the good side of a person dominates."

"You hear that, Jack?" Phil turns my way. "Just a short prick and you'll be good as new."

I back off from the gate. "Stay away from me."

"Come on, it'll be over in a second. And it will make you feel better."

"I'll feel a lot better when you open this damn gate." An odd dizziness sets in. I grab my temples, reeling against the wall. Sheesh! Dark shadows dance on the floor in front of me. "And extinguish that freaking torch," I snarl. "No one can stay sane in his head with all those wobbling shapes creeping around."

Leaning my forehead against the cold stone helps to ease the spinning carousel in my head. Deep breaths expand my chest. Yeah, that feels good. Air. Finally. Did somebody try to strangle me? Where am I anyway? A moldy odor creeps up my nose. I glance around. Oh, right, the dungeon. I think I spent the night here.

But who put me here? And why? Isn't it time to leave?

Turning around, I find three people on the other side of the gate. None of them look familiar. Have they come to visit me? Two knights and a gnome—I don't think they're family. Maybe they're here for someone else. There are probably other vaults in this cellar. Other inhabitants.

The key to my cell hangs on a hook on the wall. If

only it wasn't so far away. I stretch my arm though the gate—nope. Can't reach it.

"Hey, girl!" I whisper to the one in the red cloak. When her attention slides to me, I point at the brass keyring. "Gimme that."

She looks at my outstretched arm then back to me with a very sad face.

"Don't worry," I comfort her. "I know you're short, but it's not as high as it looks. Just stand on your toes and you'll reach it." I give her an encouraging smile. "Hurry up."

"How long will it take until it works, doctor?" the girl asks one of the other guys.

Blasted hell, is she ignoring me? "Hey, girl! The keys!" I order, a little sharper now, waggling my fingers.

"The first effect usually sets in straight away," says the dark knight with the bush-weed eyebrows. He rises from the floor and walks closer, holding a syringe in his hand.

Whoa! I jerk my arm back inside.

"It'll knock your friend out for a while. Unfortunately, there's a small side effect you need to know about," he continues. "Since this is his first time with the elixir, he might be a little keyed up after he comes to. His body and mind need to adjust. But that will go away after a few hours."

Oh no! Am I the friend he's talking about? Panic rises from my gut to my throat. "You want to knock me out?"

"No, we want to help you, Jack," answers the useless,

short scallywag in red.

How can a syringe break this vault open? I would certainly like to know that. "I'm sorry, but I believe you're mistaken. I don't know any Jack. You should try a couple cells farther down this corridor. I'm sure you'll be lucky there. Beware of the giants, though."

"We're right where we should be," the blond knight in the red shirt and white vest speaks up for the first time. He looks exhausted where he's slumped in the chair by the wall. Wearily, he leans his head back. "Just give the doc your arm. It'll all be over soon."

Backing to the far wall of the cell, I stare at them in horror. "Some shit he'll get from me."

"Buddy, listen—"

"No, wait," the dark one cuts off the blond one. "It's no use talking to him. It appears that he's already snapped and won't cooperate."

"Then what do we do now?" the girl whines, sounding really worried.

"Go home," I tell her, "and leave the key here." Hopefully, that will make her happy again. She seems like the nicest of them all.

"I had to give Tarzan a flu shot last week," the man with the syringe says in a calm voice that I don't like at all. "He was a difficult patient, too. In the end, I shot a dart at him with a blowtube."

"You think that'll work with Jack?" the girl demands, already sounding a bit happier. I'm sure it's because I told her that she can go home now.

"It should, yes," the so-called doctor assures her. "I have everything here and only need to dip the dart into the pure essence. It'll have the same effect as an injection." He fumbles with something inside his bag and then holds out a blue tube plus a small dart with bushy purple feathers. "Would any of you like to take over the shooting? I'm not very good at that sport." His forehead creases. "I had to chase Tarzan around the house for half an hour until the seventh dart finally hit its target."

"I'll do it," the red gnome volunteers and reaches for the items the dark one holds out. She fits the dart into the tube and sets it to her lips, turning toward me.

"Hold it!" I shout, lifting my hands in defense. My tongue dries out inside my mouth.

"Sorry, Jack." Again, lines of worry mar her pretty face. She's not really going to—

Whump!

A brief sting over my heart draws my gaze down. There's a ball of purple fluff sticking out of my chest, the needle penetrating my skin. "Huhhh." Pulling out the dart, I examine it for a moment, then I lift my head. All three people look at me in expectant wonder, but my words are meant for the girl alone. "I can't believe you shot me."

None of them says anything. They just stare as if they're waiting for me to turn into a Pop-Tart. And then a strange sizzle starts in my toes, rapidly creeping up my body. It feels like bugs are crawling through my veins. Shit, what is that?

The sensation intensifies twenty times when it reaches my throat. My tongue sticks to the roof of my mouth, my eyes grow wider and wider until they feel like balloons inside my skull, and the next second, I explode into the Wolf.

Boy… That hurt.

The world looks like it tipped to the side. What the freak show! They drugged me? I'm sure they snitched some of the Caterpillar's tobacco and administered it intravenously to me. Stupid people! Wanting to leap at them, I realize my right side rubs against something. Stone. The floor? Fuck, I'm lying down.

My legs row in the air as I struggle to get to my feet. It's hard work, but I'm the master. I can do anything. *Yeah, right, people! Didn't think I'd survive your conniving attack, did you?*

Once in an upright position again, I'm confronted by the next problem. The earth is quaking. Yikes, how does one stand in this rickety vault? Hastily clawing the concrete, I try to balance myself from the tremor. Still, I keep tripping over. My vision blurs. And damn, is it warm in here?

My knees are so weak, I can't hoist myself up anymore, can only lean forward. I try to reach the gate but fall again. My muzzle dunks into a steel bowl of water.

Help! Help! I'm drowning!

Because my head is so heavy, I can't seem to pull

myself out of there. Hysterically, I pedal at the bowl with my forepaws. More water splashes on my face. I squeeze my eyes shut but, thankfully, I can breathe again in the next moment. *Yeah, good. I'm safe. And still alive.*

Rolling my eyes to the people on the other side of my prison, I let my tongue loll out between my canines.

There, you wisenheimers! Couldn't kill me, huh? You'll have to come up with something stronger if you want to knock me out.

And then everything goes dark.

*

Whoa. My head hums. Feels like it's housing a swarm of bees. I lick my dry lips. Fangs… Okay, the Wolf is out. But where am I? Doesn't seem like my bed—too hard for that. And Riley wouldn't be lying in it with me either. She must be around somewhere, though, because I can hear her soft murmurs.

I have no idea what she's saying, though. Her voice comes from far away. And yet she's close because her captivating scent crowds my nose. Morning dew and wood strawberries. Unmistakable.

A funny sensation overrides the buzz in my head. It's there, right behind my ear. Like tiny squirrel feet scurrying through my fur. This feels nice—although I doubt any sane rodent would voluntarily run over a wolf.

The tiny feet remain in one place, starting a gentle

tread. I groan in pleasure.

A girlish snicker follows. "Yeah, you like that, don't you?"

Oh. So the dulcet caress comes from Riley's fingers. Is she trying to find a trigger to open my skullcap and let the bees out? That would be awesome.

My eyelids feel too heavy to lift, but I scoot a little closer to where her voice comes from. A scraping sound erupts as my paws drag over stone. Nope, *definitely* not my bed. Not even my apartment, judging by the moist, tomb-like air filtering through my nose. When my snout knocks into something hard, my eyes finally open.

I can see Riley. She's sitting on the stone floor in the warm light of a flame. But some sort of iron grid separates us. What the hell? Her arm is through one of the many square gaps, and she continues the gentle rub behind my ear.

Rolling my eyes from one side to the other, I scan my surroundings. Stone walls but no windows, a pallet in the corner, and the contorted face of a wolf staring back at me from the stainless steel of a tipped-over water bowl on the floor. Goodness, I know where I am!

Startled, I jump to my feet—or try to. The result is pancake á la wolf.

"Easy there, Jack," Riley says in a strangely soothing tone that I don't recall ever hearing from her before. "You've been unconscious for several hours."

Finally, fighting gravity, I manage to sit up. We're at

eye level now, and she smiles through the gate. "You should take it slow. I don't know if you remember what happened, but you've had a pretty tough day."

Tough day? *I remember that you shot me, little miss!* Since I came here and asked Phil to lock me up in the first place, they probably had a good reason to do it, though.

"I guess it's safe to let you out now." Riley scrambles to her feet and straightens her dress under the long, red cloak. "Can you change back to yourself?"

I will myself to change into my human body. Nothing happens. My muscles tensing, I strain harder to summon the change. Still, the Wolf remains strong. Crap, why is that?

A skeptical V appears above her nose. "Are you trying, Jack?"

No, I'm hatching an egg here. What does she think?

Freaked out, I stand up and look under my belly through my legs. Shit, there's fur everywhere. How is that possible? I never had any trouble changing to either of my forms before.

"Okay, don't panic," Riley quickly says, holding out her spread fingers to me. "Before Dr. Jekyll left, he said something like this might happen." Hanging on to the gate, she lowers to a squat and looks me in the eyes through the gaps. "He was surprised that you popped into the Wolf after the injection anyway. Since this was your first shot of Hyde elixir, it'll take a few hours for you to adjust. Don't worry. You won't be stuck in wolf form forever."

Oh, great, they drugged me with monster potion. Anything else I need to know?

She tilts her head to the side, her gaze softening. "Are you hungry?"

My tongue rolls out, and I start to pant.

Hey! Sucking it back inside, I close my mouth and frown.

"Okay." She stands. "Phil left a while ago to finish off the thing with Aurora. I don't want to go raiding through their fridge uninvited, so how about you and I go on a little hunt through the woods? The doctor said that would be okay now. Maybe we'll find a bunny for you. Or some warthog."

My ears stand at attention, and again, my tongue flaps out. Sheesh, I didn't want to do that. But what's more, my backside begins to wiggle. I check behind me to see what's going on and find my tail wagging. *Hey, stop that, you stupid, useless thing!*

Bending, I try to snatch it with my mouth, but my teeth bite into air. I struggle to lean back a little farther. *There! There! On my way!* I snap again, but every time I think I get it, my hind legs move of their own accord, and I miss it by inches. I'm chasing my tail around myself until Riley's fit of laughter makes me stop abruptly.

Hey, just so we're clear, I'm not one of those hyped-up pups, too stupid to know it's not their own tail, okay? I'm just trying to make it stay still. Totally different thing.

Still cheerfully shaking with laughter, Riley grabs the

keys from the wall and unlocks the gate. "C'mon, boy, come out! Before you get giddy in there." She slaps her thigh. I swear I can do nothing about the squeal that escapes me as I jump around her in sheer excitement, my tongue lolling out. *Fuuuck!*

Taking the torch from the wall, she leads the way out, running her fingers through the fur on the top of my head as I struggle to calm myself beside her.

As we trot out into daylight, it feels as if I've been kept underground for days. Which probably was the case. Head lifted, I draw in a really deep breath. Holy Gingerbread Man, what a delight! Until the rays of the late-morning sun tickle my nose, and I sneeze. Twice.

"Come on, you big, bad puppy dog," Riley teases me and starts running across the meadows of Castle Grove toward the forest. Immediately, I sprint after her, and when I catch up with the rolling red bundle and nudge her bottom with my snout, her laughter echoes across the lowlands.

Behind the borders of the forest where the light is cooler and darker, her jog slows to a gentle stroll. She clearly has to catch her breath from giggling so much. While I take a deep drink from the little stream beside the path, Riley plucks an apple from a tree and tosses it a few times into the air, always catching it smoothly again with one hand.

As we amble on together, my gaze remains transfixed on the fruit. She doesn't bite into it, just keeps throwing it into the air. Hopefully, it'll drop. Then it's mine.

"What?" she coos, smiling down at me. Her hand with the apple lowers in front of my nose. "You want this?"

Feverish, I skip in front of her. *Yes! Yes! Yes! Yes! Yes!*

Her grin gets wider as she hauls back her arm. "Okay, go fetch!" The next second, she pitches the fruit forward, straight into the woods, and then pulls her arm behind her back.

Holy moly! I whirl around, sprinting three steps forward. Then I stop, my gaze darting to the underbrush. Eyes wide, my heart races, but instinct makes me shoot back to Riley, and I prance before her. *Did you throw it? Did you throw it?* Frowning, I glance at the bushes again. I didn't hear it land. *Come on, you still have it behind your back, right? Do you? Do you?* Exhilarated, I snoop inside her cloak. *Where is it?*

"Oh my Goodness, Jack!" Riley falls to the ground and rolls with laughter. And there is the apple, still in her hand. I knew it!

"You'll probably want to kill me for this when you finally get back to your senses," she chirps between her giggly hiccups, "but you really should see yourself right now!"

Ha, ha. Very funny. I step over her and lick her face.

"Ew! Lay off! You're disgusting!" Dropping the fruit, she shoves at my head with both hands, turning her face away. It won't help her. She gets a proper licking. And if she laughs any harder, I might have to give her mouth-to-mouth, too.

But then a rustle in the bushes raises my hackles, and I lift my head.

Riley stops pushing at me and tilts her head, too. "What is it?"

Shh.

"Jack?"

Shhhh!

There! Something moved between the hazels. All my senses on high alert, I wait another second for the next rustle, then I sprint forward, targeting whatever is hiding in the thicket.

It smells of deer. And it's got antlers. *Boah!* An elk! Am I a lucky bastard or what?

Panic-stricken, the elk bleats as I catch it from the side and run it over. We roll across the moss until I'm on top again, holding it down with my paws. Okay, it's smaller than I thought. Maybe not an elk. But a fine meal anyway.

"Jack? Where are you?" Riley's voice drifts through the bushes shortly before she emerges. Dusting some weeds off her body, she walks forward with a proud smile. "Ah, you caught yourself a—" The smile disappears.

Why does she look so serious now?

Coming closer, her shocked gaze lights on my prey. "Is this Rudolph?"

A reindeer? Yeah, from the stark smell, it might be one. *But don't worry, we'll roast it over the fire, and it'll taste wonderful.*

"Goodness gracious! You can't eat one of Santa's reindeers!"

Why not? He's got enough of them.

"Jack! Let him go! This is Rudolph. *The* Rudolph!"

You call it Rudolph. I call it lunch.

Riley taps her foot with impatience. Whining, I shake my head, still holding on tightly to the struggling furball beneath me. She's wrong anyway. This isn't Rudi, it's probably just some guy named Matt or something. Reindeer are thick around these parts.

When its nose starts to glow, I inconspicuously cover it with my paw.

Folding her arms over her chest, Red Riding Hood coughs vigorously. "Ja-ack!"

OKAY! Rolling my eyes, I roll off the deer and sit back on my haunches. Disgruntled, the animal blows in my face before it tootles off.

My stomach growls with hunger. Great.

At least, the sound isn't lost on Riley. Her face softens, and she rubs behind my ear. Mmh, that feels amazing. Grunting in happiness, I squeeze my eyes shut and press my head into her palm. Wait! Should I be doing that?

Ah, what the hell…

"Come on, you bad puppy." She laughs. "Let's visit Granny and see if she's got food in her fridge."

My behind rises, and my tail excitedly starts flapping again. *Ugh.* Snorting, I hang my head. This time, however, I refuse to chase that traitorous part of me.

Riley eats the apple while I trot alongside her. Granny's house *does* sound good, after all. At the crossing, where we usually meet at the beginning of our story, we head in her grandmother's direction. Some movement from that part of the forest captures my attention. A small form ambles toward us, sporting yellow fur, boots, a vest, and a hat.

My eyes glaze over with delight.

Can't say that the Puss in Boots feels exactly the same joy at seeing me. His eyes grow as big as chicken eggs, and the fur on his arched back stands on end. He screeches in terror, claws shooting out.

The next instant, the cat whirls about and dashes off into the underbrush. Heck, if that isn't an invitation.

Be right back!

Chapter 9

Riley

"Jack! Leave the Puss alone!" Dang this rollicking Wolf. Dr. Jekyll's serum really did what it promised. I rub my hands over my face and cut a helpless glance at the sky. If one whelp is this much work, now I understand why Mother Goat always looks so exhausted when she takes her seven kids to town.

As the cat screeches cease in the distance, I believe Jack chased the poor guy up a tree. Thank the fairies wolves can't climb that well. Continuing on my way to Granny, I put my fingers between my lips and whistle sharply. "Jack!

Come here, boy!"

After the next two whistles, the stray puppy finally emerges from the dark side of the forest, ambling toward me across the wood anemone with his nose in the flowers as if he needs to sniff his way back to me. "Did you give the poor cat a heart attack?" I ask rebukingly, folding my arms over my chest when he comes to a halt in front of my feet.

The Wolf pulls in his lolling tongue, and I swear his lips lift in a smirk.

"Instead of chasing clueless Fairyland inhabitants, you should try to change back before the Huntsman comes after you."

The sandalwood-colored fur on his forehead crinkles in an uneasy frown. Through pursed lips, he lets out a yip. Then he squeezes his eyes closed and flattens his ears. I'm waiting for the big pop, but still, nothing happens. We both sigh, and he hangs his head in defeat.

"Nah, don't worry," I tell him and rub behind his ear because I know it'll lift his mood again. "In a few hours, the spell should be over anyway. Do you know what the doctor also said while you were zonked out?" I start walking again. Jack curiously lifts his muzzle to me. "He's confident the serum will affect you for quite a while. Like two weeks or something. Maybe even through the entire month. Which means, you won't be troubled by the pull of the story any longer."

At that news, he perks his ears. The hopeful gleam in his eyes is cute.

"Yeah, isn't it great?" I move in front of the Wolf, taking a few steps backward, and smile down at him. "In that time, I'm sure to find Prince Right For Me, we'll fall in love with each other, and once the story of Red Riding Hood is—" I hesitate and then start whispering, "B-R-O..." Warily, I quirk my eyebrows and finish my incomplete spelling by breaking an imaginary stick with my hands. "Then you won't feel any kind of calling ever again and won't have to lock yourself in other people's dungeons anymore."

It's too risky to really speak the sentence out loud. There's only one way to get out of a story, and that is by saying the words: *"I'm breaking from my tale."* Nobody really knows what happens to Fairyland residents who have no story to tell anymore. But rumor has it, there's a group of breakers dwelling on the outskirts of Oz. According to the Scarecrow, they have no home, no jobs, nothing to do or care about. Must be quite a dreary life.

Of course, that fate isn't awaiting Jack, no matter how panicky he stares at my hands currently. Once I have my prince, we'll find Jack a beautiful princess, too. New stories—happy endings.

Granny's house is around the next bend. Mother Holle steps out through the small gate in the low, coffee-brown picket fence, beaming when she lifts her head and spots us. The rotund woman wearing a white apron over her dark-blue dress is one of my grandmother's best friends. She always braids her brown hair up in two circlets over her ears. Her chubby cheeks dent as she takes my chin in her hand with a smile. "Good morning, dear child. Your grandma will be so happy to see you. She's been worried sick the past couple of days."

"Um…yes. Another adventure came in between." I scrunch my face. "Is she okay? I mean, she didn't turn into a…er…"

"Vindictive witch because you two didn't come to play?" Mother Holle finishes my sentence.

"Yeah, something like that."

She laughs and pats my shoulder. "Don't worry, sweetheart. I think your grandma actually enjoyed the vacations."

Oh. That's good. I nod. She acknowledges Jack with a tilt of her head, and we both stand there for a moment, watching the fine trail of snow falling in her wake as she leaves. I wonder how she does that.

When a cold snout nudges my hand, I emerge from my daze and let Jack through the fence gate. Before we even knock, Granny opens the door. She must have seen us coming through the window. A warm smile on her face, she welcomes us with a hug for me and a skeptical frown for Jack.

We see each other so often, I barely ever come to visit between the tales. With Jack Wolf at my side, it must look rather odd to her.

"Since you're not alone, I believe this isn't an official visit?" she asks, raising one graying eyebrow.

"No, Granny, it's not." I push my hood down and take a seat at the kitchen table. Inside, her little house looks a lot like mine. All wooden walls and cozy ambiance. I've always loved coming here.

Completely different from Mother Holle, my grandmother has the petite proportions of an imp rather than a teapot. She barely reaches my height, which is a shame because I'm already not the tallest girl on the block. But she probably doesn't mind. What she lacks in stature, she makes up for with her loving personality and humor.

"Now, tell me what kept you two away from my house for so long," she demands, placing a glass of raspberry juice in front of me and a bowl of water on the floor for the Wolf, who sits down and gives her a wary furry frown.

She rubs his head before tightening the cord of her pink terry robe and lowering into a chair across from me. Her elbows braced on the table, she plants her chin in her cupped hands, waiting curiously for me to fill her in.

I brief her about my intentions to find a prince and the weird adventures the past couple of days held for Jack and me. When she hears about the mishap with King Arthur, she almost falls off the chair from her laughter. "You really tried to shoot him out of his story? With an arrow of love?" Her salt-and-pepper hair fans out around her head on the table when she drops her forehead to her arms, sheepishly hiding her red face from me.

"All right, you can stop laughing now, Granny," I grumble.

Half a minute passes before she gets a grip again. She rises and walks to the cupboards, shaking her head at Jack with a reprimanding smile. "And you let her do that? A fine Wolf you are." Opening the fridge, she throws a quick glance back at me. "Are you hungry? I'm going to make soup and roast chicken for lunch. Jack looks like he's starving."

The sound of a decent meal makes my stomach skip with joy, so I nod, and Jack's tail starts drumming an excited tune on the floor.

"You know, the night after our encounter with King Arthur, Jack got into real trouble," I continue. "The call of the wood seems to be harder on him with his wolf half than it is with me." Taking a sip of my juice, I study Granny with a curious look. "Mother Holle said that you enjoyed your time off. So didn't you feel the pull of the tale at all?"

Giggling, she takes some veggies from a rack and gets out a big pot to put them in. "Oh, I felt it, indeed. But it was more like a funny tickle in my toes." Her puffy, pink slippers waggle. "Nothing to worry about. To be frank, I was hoping that maybe you two might like to pause the tale a little longer. When you didn't come and sent the stork to me with your message, I told Roland, and he decided to go on a cruise aboard the Nautilus."

"The Huntsman is on vacation?"

"Yes. He left last night. They're going to visit Poseidon in Atlantis, too. The journey will probably take a couple of days. I was thinking, maybe I could visit my cousin Wilma in Bedrock in the meantime."

"What a lovely idea!" I set my glass on the table and rise. From the corner drawer, I grab a vegetable peeler and head to the sink with the square window above. Red-and-white-plaid curtains are drawn back, letting in the noon sunlight. On the draining board, I find some carrots and start peeling them for the soup. "It must be a while since you've last been there."

"True. You two have been keeping me on my toes." She snickers behind me. "Wilma has been writing and asking for me to come for years. Traveling isn't so easy for her with the baby and the dinosaur, as you know. And then they only have this funny foot-work car. I can't wait to get into—" She goes abruptly quiet.

"Get into what?" I chuckle. But there's no answer. A half-peeled carrot in my hand, I turn around. My smile fades. "Granny?"

The spot where she stood only moments ago is empty except for her fluffy pink slippers. My gaze drops to the Wolf sitting beside them. The happy spark in his dark eyes makes me nervous. "Jaaack?"

Innocently, he lifts his brows.

Cocking my head, I glare at him. "Did you eat my granny?"

He shakes his head so fast, it's a miracle he doesn't get dizzy from it. He can go play the sweet puppy dog for someone else today. The bulges in his belly convict him.

"Dang it, Jack, you heard what she said! The

Huntsman is gone for several days. There's no one here to cut her out now." Grimly, I point the carrot at him. "How could you?!"

When he pulls a dog pout, I toss the veggie into the sink and grab Granny's wooden spoon instead. The part when Roland pulls out his knife and slices the Wolf's stomach still gives me chills even after living through it thousands of times. I'm certainly not going to grab a knife and do the same to save my granny.

But she must come out of there somehow.

"Open your mouth," I command, locking gazes with Jack.

Instantly, he backs away into the corner of cupboards, looking at me as if I'm the Grinch taking all his Christmas presents away. A small, helpless moue seals his lips shut.

I don't have time for this. And Granny doesn't either. "You asked for it, puppy dog." Grabbing his snout, I push my fingers and thumb into his flews until his jaws unclamp. Jack rears back with all four legs, his claws scraping on the floor, but it won't help him. As soon as there's just a tiny crack between his lips, I stuff the back end of the wooden spoon through and poke it deep down his gorge.

His eyes fly open so wide that a squirrel ogles them for a potential new home from outside the window. At the same time, he begins to gag and heave. Good. I poke harder. In a wild panic, he paws at me, but I'm not going anywhere before he throws up my gran.

When his eyes glaze over like dark crystals, and his throat works frantically, I pull out the spoon and jump back. His entire body jerks, his muscles contracting violently. He coughs and huffs for long seconds. Finally, poor Granny hurtles out of his mouth on a slide of saliva, landing on her butt on the floor. She wipes her icky-wet strands of hair away from her beaming face. "Wow! What a ride!"

I want to rush to her aid, but Jack's continued convulsive choking holds me back. He shudders and spits out a ball of buff fur right into Granny's lap. As the salivated little lump of fluff unfurls into a cat with boots, a vest, and a hat, my chin smacks my chest.

"What have you done?" a hoarse whisper escapes me. But the first round of ranting goes to the Puss in Boots.

"How dare you eat me, you stupid, fat dog?" he blusters in a foreign accent, climbing off my Granny and shaking the spittle from his fur. "Did your mama not teach you respect?" Furious, he stalks up to Jack until they're face-to-face. The nervous whimper can't save the Wolf now. "I hope you caught the kitty flu. And fleas that will drive you crazy," the Puss rages on, "by pinching and nipping you from the inside forever!" Filled with disgust, he lifts his arms. Wolf drool still drips from his hands. Yuck, I'm quite sure he doesn't want to lick that dry.

He huffs at Jack one last time and, with a swift wipe of his paw, brings his claws across Jack's face. The pained yowl makes me wince. Then the buff cat whips around on his heels and trudges out through the door. It slams shut behind him, but the ongoing scolding carries in through the windows until the Puss disappears into the forest.

Jack looks as if he just stepped off a spinning carousel. As I help my grandma up, I cut him a sharp scowl, even if the red streaks across his muzzle tear at my heartstrings. "Don't look at me like that. You know you deserved it."

A sad whine escapes him. He ducks his head and reels out of the kitchen, curling up in front of the couch.

"I better take a quick shower," Granny says, still quite amused as she hurries into the bathroom. I take the time to wipe the dog drool from the floor with a wet mop. Nothing but trouble with this Wolf. Oh, by the fen fires, it'll be such a blessing to have him back on two legs again.

After rinsing the drool off the mop and storing it away in the closet, I cut a glance to the living room. Mournful eyes glisten up from under the coffee table. The scratches on his face are gone. Wolves heal fast in Fairyland. And they need to since their stomachs are regularly cut open.

I snort at him and then return to peeling the veggies for lunch.

*

Three chimes from the grandfather clock in the living room tell us that it's a quarter to noon. Granny and I are almost finished with lunch. I take two plates out of the cupboard to set the table. As I turn around, Jack leans in the doorway. I don't know how long he's been standing there, hands in his pockets, chin bashfully lowered, and watching me from under his dark lashes.

For a split second, I halt in my tracks. A smile tugs the corners of my mouth up. Then I put the plates down and run to him, not stopping until my body crashes against his as I fling my arms around his neck. Standing on my toes, I whisper with relief into his ear, "Welcome back."

Jack wraps his arms around me, rather loosely at first. But soon enough, a deep sigh escapes him, and the embrace tightens. I close my eyes. He pulls me hard against him and lowers his forehead to my shoulder.

"Tough day, hm?" I ask.

As if too ashamed to speak, he only nods into the crook of my neck.

"Ah, what have we here?" Granny cheers from the other side of the kitchen. "The swan turned back into the princess."

Jack stiffens at the taunt, but I giggle anyway. Releasing me, he finally comes farther into the room. "Ma'am…" His voice raspy and shy, he still can't seem to hold his head as high as he usually does. "Sorry for eating you."

Yep, the past forty-eight hours put a dent in his ego. A deep one.

"Ah, don't worry, my dear." She pokes him in the side and snickers. "It was hardly the first time, now was it?"

He stares at her for a long moment, then he shakes his

head as an embarrassed grin takes shape.

"Sit down." I push him toward a chair before grabbing a third plate from the cupboard. "Lunch is ready. You must be hungry."

Granny dishes out soup for all of us, and we partake of a delicious roast chicken with gravy and tiny potato dumplings. I only wish Jack wasn't so pensive. He barely contributes to our conversation. Whenever I cast him a glance across the table, his guarded gaze is fixed on me as he silently chews chicken bits or spears chopped veggies with his fork.

"Is your friend always this quiet?" Granny voices my concern.

"Not quite so much," I reply truthfully with a touch of longing for the good old times between Jack and me.

"You know," she speaks to him now, "most of the time, I only get to see your big mouth and you from the inside. It's nice to have the real you sitting at my table for once. Feeding you"—she grins—"with something other than myself."

I nearly choke on my dumpling and look up just in time to see a tiny smile race across Jack's face. Apparently, that wasn't enough for Granny because she puts her knife and fork down and wipes her mouth with a linen napkin. "Hey, did I tell you kids that I was at P. Sherman's dental surgery last week? He made me a set of false teeth."

Now we both glance at her in confusion. This is odd. She still has all her good chompers. "What for?" Jack asks the question that's on my tongue, too.

Mischief makes her green eyes gleam as she pokes her finger cheekily into his ribs and waggles her head like a daisy in the wind. "The better to eat you with, eh?"

Dropping the cutlery, I cover my mouth with my fist, trying not to spew veggies across the entire table from laughing. The smile on Jack's face grows into a lovely chuckle. His eyes quickly dart to my side of the table before he lowers his gaze again and…holy howl of a werewolf, is that a blush on his cheeks?

It's so cute, I can't stop staring.

Of course, Jack notices it and presses his lips together in an embarrassed grin as his gaze finds me once more through those roguish strands of hair. Amazing. There seems to be so much more to this Wolf than I thought all these years.

I force myself to continue eating, but the sweet image will be forever burned into my memory.

Chapter 10

Jack

On the doorstep, Riley hugs her grandmother goodbye and wishes her a hearty bon voyage to Bedrock. The old lady waves until we close the fence gate and take the shadowed path to Glitter Hollow. This time, the birds sing happily again as we pass under the trees. I missed their chirping when we came here earlier. The forest is always quieter when the Wolf is out.

Infected by the lighthearted mood at lunch and the merry sounds of the woods now, I cheerfully bump Riley's shoulder. "I didn't know you could cook so well."

She throws a saucy grin back at me. "And I didn't know you were so deeply in love with your tail."

Yeah, that was clear. It had to come out now that it's just the two of us again. I roll my eyes and pull the hood of her cloak over her head, snorting, "I don't normally chase my own tail. You *know* that, Red Riding Hood."

She peeks at me from under the fabric. Her eyes sparkle with a smile, and the sight suddenly holds a beauty I can barely grasp. She's always been pretty to me when she looks at me so shyly in the tale. But we aren't following a storyline here, acting something out. This is different. It's sincere. The *real* Riley I haven't seen before.

"Pity I had no camera with me," she teases. "You were the cutest pup in the world."

"I had drugs pumped into me," I mutter through clenched teeth. But the smile is hard to keep away from my face. "Next time, someone should knock *you* out with Jekyll's serum." Throwing an arm around her, I tickle her side and pull her closer.

"Jack!" she squeals and almost trips. Pushing away from me, she bats her lashes rapidly in sweet innocence. "Will you sit with me all through the night and rub behind my ear, too?"

A deep growl rolls in my throat. Riley interprets it perfectly and takes a wary step backward even though her eyes gleam excitedly, and the corners of her mouth twitch. Heck, after last night, scaring this girl has probably become a whole lot harder. It doesn't mean I can't chase her to the other side of the forest, though. My lips curve up. She doesn't need more warning than that. Her giggles echo through the woods as she whirls about and dashes away. Three seconds of a head start is what she gets, and then I bolt after her.

The woods are her home. Too easily, she finds her way out of the forest and sprints through Duckburg right down to the Swan Lake. The giant chestnut tree by the lakefront not only provides a shadowy shelter to a small group of frogs there, but it obviously looks like a good shield to Riley, as well. She slips behind the trunk and peeks out to check which side I'm coming from. "Give up! You'll never get me, Jack!" she shouts.

Slowing to a prowling gait, I lower my chin, fixing her with a predatory gaze. "Oh, how wrong you are, Red Riding Hood."

For a second, she disappears behind the tree, only to peer out from the other side, giggling. "And what will you do if you catch me? Blow me down like the first little pig's house?"

Hmm, she gives me an idea here. My chest swells with a mighty breath, and the exhale hits her like a squall. This is something all Fairyland wolves have down pat. Squeezing her eyes shut, she ducks her head and grips the tree for support. Her cloak flaps until the button at her throat pops, and the red satin scatters in the wind along with a handful of frogs before the whole lot lands in the grass near the water.

When the blast ebbs off, she looks at me with new awe in her eyes. The cheeky smile, however, I couldn't wipe off her face. "Is that all you can do, big, bad puppy dog?"

I cock my head. "Do you really think it wise to tease a wolf? One blow and your cloak vanished." As I stalk closer, the left side of my mouth lifts into a sneer. "Another…and you'll stand in front of me butt-naked."

Her cute mouth shapes into a perfectly round O. "You wouldn't!"

Ever so slowly strolling closer, I fix her with a challenging stare. "You want to try me?" Oh, I hope she does because right now, there are so many things I'd like to do with her.

"No!" Riley squirms away and hides behind the tree. I guess it doesn't matter anymore which side I come to attack her from. I go for the opposite one from where she just disappeared, hoping that she'll run right into my arms. Well, she doesn't, and I have to chase her around the chestnut, which I don't mind doing because her pony-like snicker is the sweetest thing I've heard today.

We switch directions every so often, but the little weasel is too quick, always grinning back at me…just out of reach. This will go on until sunset unless I change my strategy soon. So, when Riley slides around the trunk again, I take the chance and jump, grabbing onto a thick branch above my head. Swiftly, I hoist myself up, crouch there, and wait.

Two seconds later, she peeks around the tree, hands

braced against the trunk. I hold back my chuckle and quietly watch her as she goes looking for me.

"Jack?" Her voice is soft, teasing, and full of cockiness. "Where are you?" Soon enough, it dawns on her that she won't find me behind the tree, and she steps away, scanning the area around her. Because she's right beneath my branch, I tighten my grip and lower myself soundlessly to the grass behind her.

Leaning in just a little bit to get closer to her ear, I whisper. "Miss me already, honeydrop?"

Riley shrieks, and I swear she jumps three feet into the air. My intent was to catch her in an embrace before she made another dash for escape, but I can't because I'm laughing so hard that I need to grab on to the tree for support.

"Ha. Ha," she snorts, staking me with a scowl. "You're so funny."

"No, *you* are." Still laughing, I take her hand and drag her with me to the lakeshore where her red cloak is spread out in the sun. Instead of picking it up, Riley lowers onto the grass, and so do I. She plucks a blade and jams it between her thumbs, cupping her hands around it as she lifts it to her mouth. The creaking sound when she blows into her makeshift instrument tortures my eardrums, and not just because of my supersensitive hearing. Even the swans paddle away across the lake to escape, and the frogs nearby simply dip underwater.

"Stop it, woman!" I whine, pressing my hands to my

ears. "Please."

The painful sound isn't lost on her, either, because she winces and, with a sheepish grin, throws the blade of grass away. Then she starts tossing pebbles into the crystal-clear water. That's a sound I don't mind.

For a long while, I watch her, quietly drinking in her unobtrusive beauty. Her amber eyes and snowy face. Her entire bearing. She appears happy, frisky, and thoughtful all at once. I suddenly realize that I just can't look away, wondering what's on her mind.

The answer to that question is given when she plucks a daisy from next to her feet and starts to pull out the little white petals one by one.

"He loves me... He loves me not... He loves me..." I taunt her, going along as she works the flower.

Riley doesn't look at me, but a smile puffs out her reddened cheeks.

The realization that she'll soon break with our tale brings a whiff of sadness once again. Even if her initial plan with Cupid's arrow didn't work out the way she hoped, plan B is already in progress. Funny, it's my best friend of all people who's going to aid Riley in her endeavor. Then again, Phil never can say no when his golden-locked love flutters her eyelashes at him. Eric and I have had discussions about it with him for ages.

Crossing my legs and bracing my forearms on my knees, I breathe in deeply and turn my head to Riley. "So...a royal ball, huh?"

Her shy gaze is the only thing that briefly moves to me. Lips compressed and gaze focused back on the flower, she nods. "Mm-hmm."

"Well—" I straighten, bracing myself on my hands behind me in the grass as I try to swallow the uncomfortable feeling in my chest without her noticing. "You've got it all covered then, don't you?"

"What do you mean?" This time, she looks at me for a bit longer. The daisy is only a stem with a yellow cup in her fingers now. I don't know the outcome of her game.

"The prince hunt. Plan A was the arrow. It failed." My right shoulder jerks in a casual shrug. "Plan B is the ball?"

She giggles, throwing stones into the water again while the bravest of the frogs climb back on land, and even a couple of swans return. "You know what, Jack? It's probably for the best that my arrow missed King Arthur. I mean, I don't know him at all, do I?" She tilts her head to me, her forehead creasing helplessly. "What if he's weird? He would have been eternally in love with me without an out-clause." She shudders and shakes her head. "It could have been quite exhausting."

I picture it for a moment and, frankly, I don't like the image. If she's going to get stuck with someone that she's not happy with for the rest of her life, we might as well stay Red Riding Hood and the Wolf.

"Better to get to know the prince before binding him to me, right?" she asks. "Like Aurora and Phillip did. And all my other friends." And then she adds in a much lower, softer voice, sounding almost insecure, "Who knows, maybe there's even someone who really likes me. Not because of a spelled arrow but simply for who I am."

"Any guy who doesn't notice the beauty in you is an idiot." The words fly out of my mouth before I even realize what I'm saying.

Riley eyes me in wonder for a second. "That's sweet of you to say," she whispers before she drops to her back and dreamily sighs as she studies the blue sky. "Maybe that special prince will even like hunting as much as I do. And reading. And jumping from roofs into haystacks. And raspberry cake." Her head tilts to my side. "Wouldn't that be wonderful?"

My eyebrows lift in amazement. "You jump into haystacks?" I haven't done that since I moved from a farm into my apartment above Geppetto's workshop years ago. Boy, do I miss it sometimes.

"Whenever I see one," she tells me gleefully. The skin around her eyes crinkles slightly as she gives me a secretive smile. "There's one right behind the old mill by the Timeless Brook in the forest."

I laugh and lay back beside her. "Ah, you better not let *any* prince see you do that. You know, it's very unprincesslike."

"But that's the whole point." Riley smacks me on the shoulder, then she rolls to her front, braces herself on her elbows, and excitedly peers down into my eyes. A silky lock lands across my face and tickles my upper lip. "My perfect prince wouldn't be stiff, wearing funny robes and sticking to etiquette twenty-four hours a day."

I blow the lock away. "He wouldn't?"

"No. He'd be funny and adventurous—"

"Not to mention extremely wealthy if he owns his own castle," I add flatly.

She giggles, but soon, her face straightens again. "He'd be friendly, too. And considerate. And very handsome, of course. Tall and muscular. His eyes would sparkle like sapphires, and his hair would be a perfect shade of gold…" Her gaze trails off toward the sky as her thoughts obviously do in her mind.

"Hey!" Playfully, I push against her shoulder just hard enough so she tips to the side and comes down from her castle in the air. "Would you please stop slobbering over Prince *If-Only-You-Were-Real* in front of me? You're doing a fine job of castrating my ego here."

Riley rips a handful of grass out of the ground and tosses it at my head, laughing hard. "As if that's even possible!"

I catch her wrist and pull her back to me. She lands on my chest, her nose touching mine. It coaxes a soft gasp from her, which sounds really cute. I wrap my arms around her and drawl, "Maybe I should keep you locked up in Rapunzel's tower until you drop the idea of this pimped version of a happily ever after."

For an extended moment, Riley lets me gaze into her stunned honey-hued eyes before her expression softens to something that almost looks like pleading. "But you're supposed to help me find it. Don't you want to anymore?"

This particular look reminds me a lot of Aurora and Phillip.

Fuck.

I expel a deep breath and help her off me. As we both sit upright again, I run my knuckles across her cheekbone, skimming a few wisps of hair back and tucking them behind her ear. "Only joking. Of course, I'm going to help you."

Slowly, she blinks a couple of times, tilting her head slightly to one side. And there it is—the smile no guy in this world can say *no* to. "So, will you come with me to the ball and help me look for a prince?"

"No!"

Her perfectly wing-shaped eyebrows crinkle into a dumbfounded V as she pulls her head back. "Why not?"

We can stop playing our tale if it makes her happy, but hell if I'm going to stand back and watch her replace me with some royal douche. That's why! "I'm not a prince."

"And I'm no princess. But that's the whole point." Her gaze keeps me captured. "You could find a princess there."

"I don't want a princess. Anyway, I've got other plans for Friday night."

"Really? What?" Her disappointment vanishes, and an impish waggle of her eyebrows takes over. "Do you have a date?"

Lips compressed, I let a frustrated snort out through my nose as I hang my head and slide a scowl her way.

"What?"

"I think you need to stop going to the regular princess meetings. They must be adding something to the tea there. Completely clouding your brain with too much romance."

Riley sticks out her tongue at me and then grabs her cloak, loosely draping it around her shoulders because the button at the collar is now gone. She smirks. "You're just jealous because I'm going to find my prince on Friday, and you probably have something like laundry to do."

Irritated, I pull the hood up over her head again, but deeper over her face this time. It's easier to stay angry with her when those cute eyes and smile are covered. Or…maybe not. "I'll do the laundry tonight to be free for an adventure on Friday."

She brushes the hood back so she can turn her bright gaze on me again. "A masked ball could be an adventure."

"Nope."

"Oh, come on. You need to go, too. It'll be fun."

"Maybe for you."

"There'll be a band. Good music and nice food."

"I'll have a cheeseburger down at the pub."

"We could dance."

"I don't dance," I growl with an intense look into her eyes.

Riley gasps, covering her mouth with her hand. "Is that it? You don't want to go because you can't dance?"

Rolling my eyes, I can barely hold back a laugh. "Yes, Red Riding Hood. That's exactly the reason."

"Hey!" She shoves my shoulder, making a mean face—and terribly shipwrecks it. "Don't use your sarcasm on me."

I lean close to her ear and drawl, "Sorry, there's no one else but you here. Bear it." The scent of morning dew and wood strawberries catches me unaware, momentarily dazzling my mind. It wipes the grin off my face. With my lips so close to her neck, I want to press them gently against her skin, run my tongue over it, and find out if she only smells of this addictive odor or tastes of it, too. Instinctively, I jerk back, taking a second to shake myself out of the crazy stupor that has overtaken me.

Riley, searching my face with narrowed eyes, doesn't miss my discomfort. "Are you all right?"

"Mm-hmm." A sigh wants out, but I don't let it. "Your hair just tickled my nose. I thought I needed to sneeze." Yep, king of excuses. She should marry *me*.

A group of frogs climbs out of the water. The little green guys plant themselves in the sun next to our feet to warm up. My mind still racing with thoughts that will get me into trouble, they just might be the right distraction. I fight to get my shit together and playfully tug at one of Riley's soft locks. "You know what? Maybe you should squeeze plan F in between A and B."

Her look of concern gives way to a curious frown. "What is F for?"

"Frogs." I grin, grab one, and hold it right under her

nose. "Maybe your super prince hides inside one of these?"

Instead of grimacing and pushing away like I expected, she just folds her arms and cocks a daring eyebrow. "What? You think I won't kiss it?"

I think I would throw up if *I* had to put my lips on one of these little slimebags. Since she's so eager to meet her royal ever after, I push the frog forward a little.

Riley tucks her legs under her bottom and takes the toxic-green amphibian from me. Almost tenderly, she holds it up to her face. In a tick-tock rhythm, her gaze switches from the animal to me and back.

"Scared?" I taunt her, unsure if she really has the guts to go through with this.

Determined, she presses her lips together then puckers them and closes her eyes. Good Grimm, she can't really—

No!

My face contorts with disgust when the smack sounds out, and Riley leans back with a content expression. That, however, morphs quickly into a sullen frown. "What? You don't turn into a prince?" She presses another kiss on the amphibian's head. And another. When her efforts remain fruitless, she tosses the frog aside and grabs the next.

In a rapid mania, she kisses her way through at least seventeen of the slimy fellas. I need to duck to escape getting hit square in the face by her discards.

"*Ugh*, Riley."

My grunt breaks her mission. "What?"

"You're like a steamroller on love drugs."

A deep sigh escapes her. Still holding the latest frog in her petite hand, she drops her arm, and her face scrunches in disappointment. "What's wrong with them? Why won't they turn into gorgeous princes?"

"I don't know." I try, but I can't hold back a chuckle at her cute expression. At least it doesn't explode out as full-on laughter. "Maybe you're going for the wrong kind?"

"What do you mean?"

"Well, everybody can kiss pretty frogs, right?"

"You think a real prince would hide in an ugly toad?"

"The ugliest." Luckily, we have one right there on a rock. I pick up the warty thing and offer it to my gallant prince huntress. Her cheeks turn pale, and her eyes pop wide as she takes the toad and nearly gags.

Okay, total fail. I'm rolling on the ground, laughing.

"Oh, man, why can't princes hide behind pretty animals? Like birds," she whines. "I wouldn't mind kissing a robin."

Bravely, she puckers her lips once more but, no matter how hard she tries, she can't bring herself to kiss the toad. Every attempt ends with her face contorting, and her body shaking in revulsion. I have to wipe tears from my eyes.

"You're doing this because I stuffed the wooden spoon down your throat, right?" she murmurs.

Revenge? "Maybe…" Being forced to choke up an old woman—and a cat—was one of my less pleasant experiences this week. She deserves to be taunted a little for it. In the end, I take pity on my girl, though, and release the toad from her death-grip. "Let it go, honeydrop. There was only ever one prince that turned green, and that frog is already taken."

"But..." Her shoulders slump, and her eyebrows follow suit.

I put the toad back on the rock, take Riley's hand, and pull her up with me. As we take a shortcut home, I drape an arm around her and kid with a smirk, "If you're really so desperate to find a royal lover, you'll have to dig a hole and wait until some unlucky bastard falls into it."

Riley stops so quickly that my hand drops from her shoulders. Her suddenly exhilarated gaze locks with mine. "Say that again!"

Uh-oh. "It was a joke."

Clasping the front of my t-shirt in her small fists, she beams right up at my face. "No, Jack, you're brilliant!"

I'm not exactly sure I would call myself that right now. "You don't really want to catch a prince in a burrow, do you?"

"Of course not, silly. That would be a stupid idea." Releasing my shirt, she grabs my hand and enigmatically pulls me along the path through the trees. "How long is Geppetto's workshop open today?"

"I don't know." But from the excitement in her whole bearing, perhaps I should hope it's already closed when we get there.

Chapter 11

Riley

Thursday morning, I carry a basketful of nails, screws, rope, a screwdriver, and two hammers into the forest. Jack trudges after me, carrying the wood.

Yesterday evening when we came to Geppetto's workshop, the *Closed* sign was still swinging behind the glass in the door. We missed him by seconds. With this brilliant plan forming in my head, every hour counted, so I told Jack to meet me at the shop right at cockcrow the next morning. It took a bit of hard work to make him come when he kept rolling his eyes, but in the end, he agreed.

Most likely because he was too curious to see what I would craft today.

"Don't dawdle back there!" I call over my shoulder. "There's lots to do before this trap will be prince-fit."

"I'm a wolf, not a *drudge*," his querulous words drift to me from some twenty feet behind, followed by a low grumble of curses that I don't want to repeat.

Close to the mill near the Timeless Brook, warm sunrays break through the treetops and mark the perfect spot for my trap. With a happy sigh, I put the basket down and swirl around to Jack. He's a walking woodpile on legs. I can't see anything of him above his belly button. "Watch out!" I say quickly and step aside before he knocks me over. "You can drop it here."

A relieved grunt sounds from behind the wood. He lowers his arms, and a giant load of laths falls, tumbling to the mossy ground. With his forearm, he wipes the sweat from his face and braces his other hand against a tree trunk to catch his breath. "What do you need all this wood for? That's enough to build a house."

Not a house, but a box. A huge one. I push the hood of my cloak back. It's fastened around my neck again because, last night, I replaced the button that popped off when Jack tried to blow me naked. From the inside pocket of the cloak, I remove the plan for my genius trap, which I rather awesomely drew with some fancy crayons. Unfolding the paper, I lay it on the ground and beckon Jack over with a nod. He lowers beside me.

The picture shows some trees. "That's the woods," I point out.

It earns me a wry look from Jack. "No shit."

Ugh, he can be so unnerving in the early morning hours. "Right, so this," I explain, ignoring his grumpiness as I point a finger at the blue square in the center of the drawing, "is the bed we're going to make for the prince."

"A bed?" Jack raises one eyebrow, sitting back on his heels. Like a sulking pixie, he folds his arms across his chest. "In the forest?"

"Yeah, well…they are easier to catch when they're asleep." Why can't he just shut up and stick with my plan? It's brilliant! "If a prince is racing his horse through the woods, he might be tired and appreciate a snug place to rest for a moment. I thought of bringing my sofa out here, but a pile of pillows will do, I guess. The main point is for it to look cozy and inviting to him."

His eyes sparkle and his mouth becomes a tight curve, small dimples in his cheeks telling me how hard he's trying not to laugh. *Argh!* He waves a hand at me. "Okay, go on."

Bracing my palms on my thighs as I kneel on the ground, I lick my lips and emphasize my next words. "If you don't take this seriously, you may as well go home, and we'll eighty-six the whole plan." I nail him with a scowl. "But then you're coming to the ball with me, *and* you're going to help me pick a lover. Understand?"

"I'm sorry," he pledges, yet I know he's not because he shakes with laughter now. "Your idea is fantastic. Let's build the prince trap. So, what the hell is this?"

I follow his finger to my excellent drawing of a brown, upside-down crate. "This is what we're going to do today." Picking up a twig from beside my knee, I finger it, glancing hopefully at Jack. "We're going to build a box so big, it'll easily slide over the pillow stack *and* the slumbering prince. A mighty branch will hold up one side so it looks like a nice little roof over the camp. This rope triggers the release."

"Where will the two of us be in the meantime?"

"Right over here." I tap the twig's end on the bushes sketched on the plan, where two pairs of eyes peer out. I'd drawn a pair of pointed ears for Jack, too.

"And when the poor man hits the sack, we're going to tug on this rope, which will pull the stick away, making the whole thing snap shut."

"Exactly!" Radiant with delight, I toss away my twig. "It's foolproof."

"That remains to be seen." A chuckle still on his lips, Jack stands and holds out a hand to me. "Come on, joiner's apprentice. Let's build you a prince trap."

I climb to my feet with his help. We lay out the laths according to my plan and start screwing them together. The work actually takes longer than expected. The morning dwindles fast, the sun downright zooming across the sky.

When the last nail disappears into the wood, I drop back on my bottom and, with my cloak, wipe the sweat from my brow. "*Phew.* Finally."

Jack sits down under a tree and watches me with a smirk. "Not your kind of work, hm?"

I shake my head. As hunger makes itself known with a rumble in my stomach, I jump up and go on a raid through the basket. Hidden under all the ironware were a couple of sandwiches and a bottle of mineral water. "Hungry?" I ask Jack, holding out a snack to him.

We eat together, and when I'm done with mine, I unscrew the lid of the bottle. Apparently, leaving the basket in the sun was a bad idea because the whole thing gushes over—the gas of the mineral water having reacted to the heat. In a panicked reflex, I hold the bottle away from me so the water splashes somewhere else. On Jack, to be exact.

Even though he quickly presses his palm to the mouth of the bottle, half of the contents are already soaking his t-shirt. Drawing up my shoulders in a shrug, I give him a sheepish smile. "Oops…"

"Oops?" His eyebrows arch, daring me to come up with a better excuse for dousing him when I could have watered an entire clearing.

I have none, other than it was fun. "Yeah…oops."

Jack takes the bottle out of my hand and tosses it aside, rising like the magic beanstalk above me as his dumbfounded expression turns into a wicked sneer. "I'll give you *oops!*"

This time, there's no chance for me to dash away because he pulls me up so fast, the momentum makes me fall over his shoulder as he quickly bends. "Jack!" A hysterical shriek leaves me. The only things I see are his heels and calves as he strides over to the mill. And then the forest disappears as we're ascending some stairs in the dark. "Jack, what are you doing?"

The farther up we go, the brighter it gets inside the small, old building. The roof hatch must be open. "Let's see if this robin can fly," he answers with a smirk in his voice.

"What? You wouldn't—"

"Oh, you bet, I *so* would."

One second later, I'm airborne and screaming my lungs out. Rowing my arms and legs doesn't help. I plummet backward off the top of the mill, Jack's grin the only thing I can focus on from where he stands in the open port.

With a poof, I land on a soft surface that flattens under my weight. Grain dust rises all around me.

"Didn't you say you love jumping into haystacks?" his amused voice drifts down to me through the thick, yellow pall.

"Not like that, you maniac!" I shout, still freaked out from the drop but now also laughing.

Arms spread-eagle, Jack dives off the port. "Move!"

I have just enough time to roll to the side before he flattens me. His landing whirls up another cloud of grain dust. Waving it aside with both of my arms, I search for his face through the mist. A grin sits lazily on his lips as we lock gazes, and I start laughing again. "Anyone ever tell you that you're off the wall?"

Jack waggles his eyebrows. "Again?"

The man is simply unbelievable! I stare at him for a couple of seconds longer. Then my gaze slides to the roof hatch, and I roll off the haystack. Dashing to the mill's front door, I holler over my shoulder, "Last one up is an ogre fart."

Halfway up the stairs, I can feel him breathing down my neck.

*

The sun touches the treetops in a late-afternoon caress as Jack and I carry each and every pillow I own from my house to the place in the woods where we spent most of the day. The giant crate leaning against an oak tree for now just waits to be used. Jack suggested building a nest of hay for the prince since there was obviously enough of it behind the mill, but that wasn't what I had in mind. Instead, I made him come home with me to play drudge once more.

We arrange the pillows in a nice bed on the ground and line them with a couple of cuddly, red blankets. It's the perfect invitation for a prince, tired from a long journey.

"Now what?" Jack demands as we both stand in front of the makeshift bed, hands propped on our hips, admiring our work. "Want to put up a sign: *Prince bed this way?*"

"No." I contradict with the same humor in my voice and stick out my tongue at him. Now comes the bait. I run and pluck some strawberries from a nearby bush. Carrying them back in my cupped hands, I place them in the center of the bed.

Jack cocks his head. "You think you can lure him in with berries?"

"Yeah…I actually thought of trying apples, but then I heard they only work with wolves." I wink, unable to resist teasing him about our stroll through the forest yesterday when he wasn't quite himself. The growl he emits is obviously fake. He doesn't scare me. Not when his eyes sparkle with amusement, and certainly not when a fall from the mill roof is the worst that could happen to me again. A giggle rocks me. "Or do you like strawberries, too, puppy dog?" I grab one from the pile, haul my hand back, and then toss the berry past his left ear and into the bushes. "Go fetch!"

Jack stands rigid, the mischief in his eyes growing as he dips his chin and snarls. Next thing I know, I'm lifted off my feet as he leaps at me, and we both land in the soft nest of pillows behind me. Squealing, I try to roll away from under him, but he keeps me in a tight embrace and lowers his mouth to my ear. "Got you."

A warm shiver whizzes through me at his gentle breath against my skin. My laugh ceases, my body going still. With one arm still around me, Jack skims the fingertips of his other hand across my cheek. "No escaping…"

Only my gaze slides to his face, and I bite my bottom lip, suddenly feeling nervous. The birds and rodents must feel it, too, because the forest goes silent around us.

Rays of a golden sunset beam through the trees, lighting Jack's dark eyes as he smiles. This is weird…him so close. I have never been held by a man. Not for so long…not so tenderly. It's pleasant on a strange level. And it makes my heart pound dramatically fast.

My hands flattened against his chest, I return the smile because it feels natural to do so. Thoughts run wild in my mind. The first comes out in a shy whisper. "You sure are the craziest Wolf of your kind, Jack."

"You like crazy, Red Riding Hood," he whispers back, lowering his head to mine. His warm breath strokes across my mouth just before his lips do. It was barely a real touch, yet my body trembles from it.

Jack remains motionless and looks at me from inches away. I'd always thought touching his face would feel like getting up close and personal with a cactus because of the raggedy three-day beard he sports. Surprisingly, it doesn't. To be honest, his lips, when they brushed against mine, reminded me of a velvet raspberry. With a will of its own, my hand moves up to his mouth, my fingers lightly running across his bottom lip. "I like raspberries," the first thought slips again.

His brows furrowing in confusion, he laughs quietly. "Do you?"

I nod. And part of me wants to touch his raspberry lips

again. Maybe Jack wants it, too, because he laces our fingers as he moves our hands back to the pillow-bed beneath me, and then his gaze falls to my mouth. I close my eyes.

My heart does funny things in my chest again. Dancing, maybe skipping, I don't really know. Then a thunderous crack sounds, making me wince in Jack's arms. That was not from my heart. He jerks, too, and my eyes shoot open just in time to see a monstrous birch tumbling down. A shriek escapes me. Too late to run, I throw my arms over my head for protection and accidentally punch Jack in the chin in the process. He yips in pain, and I immediately feel sorry for doing that right before we die.

As if by a miracle, the deadly strike from the tree never comes. It misses our camp by a foot. Still in shock, I jump to my feet, dragging Jack with me. Breathing hard, I scan around to find out why trees were suddenly falling in the Wood of 1000 Dawns.

Turns out, a beaver chomped it. He's now struggling to tug the birch into the water.

"Ow." Jack rubs his jaw. "Were you trying to knock my fangs out?"

"Sorry." I cast him a sheepish glance, pleading for forgiveness. "I thought the tree was going to kill us."

Jack glares at the birch jerkily moving past us, and then he raises a provocative eyebrow at me. "Hardly."

Okay, maybe the tree wasn't that monstrous. More like a seven-foot stick with barely any branches worthy of mention. When pulled out of my moment with Jack, it did look scary, though.

And now I wonder if it was fortune that made the rodent choose to fell that particular tree next to us. If it hadn't, Jack might have stolen my first real kiss. Or…I would have given it to him.

Oh, the horror of that!

After all the hard work I put into finding a prince, that could have ruined everything. To really change my ever after and, consequently, the story, my first kiss has to be one of true love. It can't be wasted in a careless moment with a Wolf.

Feeling the heat of shame surging to my cheeks, I avoid his gaze and walk to the crate still leaning against the oak. "We should move this in place before it gets too dark."

Jack comes without another word and helps me drag the lathed box over to the pillow camp. While he holds one side up, I jam a branch as thick as my arm underneath it. Testing if the construction is windproof, he shakes it a little. After his approving nod, I tie one end of the rope to the stick and carefully lay out the rest on the ground, making sure it's covered by moss. Then we hide in the bushes.

"And what do we do now?" Jack hisses as we both lower to the ground.

Lying on my front, I brace myself on my elbows. The rope end tightly in my hand, I focus on the prince trap ahead. "Now, we wait."

Time ticks by.

The sun disappears, and somewhere in the forest, an owl starts to hoot a jolly good evening to the bright moon above. The first half hour, Jack lay dutifully beside me, keeping an eye on the latch bolt with me. But over the past few minutes, he's become fidgety. "I don't think this monstrosity is really going to work."

I place an annoyed finger in front of my lips. "Shh."

"Oh, come on, Riley." He stands, flexing his shoulders and spine. A funny string of cracks sounds out. "You can't hang out here the entire night."

Jaw set, I tilt up my head to him. "Watch me."

"You will freeze to death."

He has a point. A cold breeze picked up some time ago. It might get a little chilly tonight. But that wouldn't stop me. "I'm tough."

"You're wolf meal."

"You're the only Wolf out here, and I don't think you're going to eat me."

"Fine. Then bears."

Actually touched by his concern, I send him a soft smile. "If you're so worried about me, then stay."

He glares at me for several long seconds. "No way. If this is your idea of a thrilling night, count me out." He stomps away but, after a couple of steps, he stops. Curiously, I wait to see what sort of excuse he'll find next to try and make me go home.

Swiveling around, Jack rubs his hands over his face

and grunts at the moon. I guess I frustrate him more than fleas in his pants, but what else can I do? The trap won't snap over the prince on its own. Someone needs to sit this out, at the ready to pull the cord at the right moment.

"One hour!" Jack growls and spears me with a toxic look as he lowers back to my side. "If your prince doesn't show up in that time, we're going home. That means you, too! No further discussion. Do I make myself clear?"

"Perfectly clear." Scooting to the side to make room for him, I crack a smile because his suggestion sounds fair, and I like his company. Hanging out with a Wolf is better than getting eaten by a bear.

We remain on silent watch again. For a long time… And no prince comes by on his noble steed. Instead, the wind picks up speed, freeing leaves from the trees and bushes around me. I don't know if the hour is over because neither Jack nor I have a watch, but when the sky breaks with rolling thunder, I know he wants to go home. Moments later, the first raindrop lands on my nose. I wipe it away, my gaze still focused on the trap, but more drops follow, and they fall even faster.

As Jack finds shelter under a nearby weeping willow, I refuse to abandon ship. Just a few more minutes. I'm sure my prince will come.

The cold from the ground seeps through my dress and into my bones. Soon, my cloak is soaked with rain, too. I start to shiver.

"Riley…?" Stiff from iciness, I can barely make myself

turn in the direction of Jack's soft voice. His hand appears in front of my face, obviously waiting for me to grab it. "Come on. It's time to get you out of the rain."

A melancholy sigh escapes me as I tie the end of the rope to the root of a tree bridging out of the ground. Then I reach for Jack's hand. Gently, he helps me up and nods toward the path leading to Glitter Hollow. The idea of a cup of hot chocolate in front of a crackling fire holds unarguable appeal.

I pull up my hood and tug it down my forehead. Jack doesn't have a hood or even a jacket because he only wore his t-shirt when we met that morning. He ducks his head as we both run all the way to my house through the moonlit forest.

He stops in front of the stairs leading up to my porch, while I scurry under the awning to escape the rain. A tender goodbye looms in his gaze. "See you tomorrow."

I nod. It's so sweet that he wanted to make sure I got home safely before heading on to his own apartment.

But it's a long way to Grimmwich, and the rain is coming down in sheets now. His clothes are already drenched, as are mine. He shouldn't be walking miles through the storm tonight. So when he turns around to leave, I suck in a quick breath and insecurely call out, "Jack?"

He halts, rain dripping from his eyelashes as he looks at me over his shoulder.

"I'm going to make hot chocolate." I shrug and press

my lips together, expelling a helpless breath through my nose. "Would you like some?"

Three seconds pass. Eventually, the corners of his mouth slowly lift into a lovely smile. Mine follow suit. He comes up the few steps onto the porch, towering half a foot over me and once again standing close. Then he puts an arm around my shoulders, and together, we walk inside.

Chapter 12

Jack

We build a fire in her stove, and while Riley hangs a pot with milk above it, I take her cloak and walk outside to wring it out. With my shirt equally as wet, I pull it off and squeeze that, too, before slipping it back on. There's a small stack of chopped wood next to the door. I jam a couple of logs under my arm and bring them inside to nurture the fire, then move a chair from the kitchen table closer to the stove and hang the red cloak over the backrest to dry.

Riley's place is lovely. Small, but very homey. It's chock-full of whimsical furniture and amazing knickknacks. Everything smells like wood and, currently, a bit of smoke from the fire. But above all, the sweet scent of morning dew and wood strawberries prevails.

When we came here earlier in the afternoon to collect the pillows for the prince bed, there was hardly time to look around. Now, it feels as if the little house speaks to me, beckoning me to touch the flowered curtains and run my fingers across a sloping chest of drawers. Picking up the clock there, my mouth curves into a small smile when I realize it's ticking backward.

"A present from Alice," Riley's gentle voice sounds from behind me. "I think she got it in Wonderland."

I put the clock back on the chest and turn to her. The steaming white mug she holds out to me looks enticing. My fingers brush hers as I reach for it, and it reminds me of our moment in the forest. "Why have we never hung out before?" I asked her, tilting my head and searching her face. "Outside our tale, I mean. Why haven't we gone for coffee or visited each other at home?"

She pulls back her hand, grabbing her own mug and shyly dropping her gaze to the drink. "I guess we see each other so much in the story that it just never seemed necessary."

She has a point. After spending seven to eight hours each day on the job together, everyone probably just goes their own way—unless they're married and live in the same castle.

Even if her wanton idea of changing our fairy tale fate

still gives me the creeps, at least a tiny good thing came out of it. With a finger under her chin, I lift her face and wait until she looks at me again. "It was nice getting to know the real you these days, Red Riding Hood."

A shy smile appears on her lips, and she nods slightly.

Since there are no cushions or blankets left on the couch after our earlier raid, I sit down on the cuddly grizzly bear skin in front of the fire. Leaning against the sofa, I tilt my head back, look up at her, and pat the place next to me on the floor. With a grin, she follows my invitation and settles down on the shaggy rug beside me.

The fast-rising temperature in the log cabin dries our clothes within minutes. My jeans and t-shirt soon feel as if they've been ironed on my body. The hot drink burns down my throat and further warms me from the inside.

Her heels pulled to her bottom, Riley keeps her fingers wrapped around the steaming mug in her lap. Golden flames dance in her big amber eyes. Her sweet snub nose twitches, and she sniffs. I wonder what's on her mind as she stares so quietly into the fire.

Her rain-soaked strands have dried to beautiful chestnut-colored locks again. I didn't touch them often in the past, but this week, I have. I know how silky soft they feel. They call to me, beckoning me to wrap them around my fingers and play. But I can't do that. Or can I?

Ah, what the hell… Under the pretext of scratching my neck, I plant my elbow on the couch behind her head.

"Jack?" Her soft voice makes my hand freeze and

hover mere inches from her hair. She hesitates before speaking again. "It *was* really nice spending the past couple of days with you. But…what happened back there in the forest…it can't happen again."

Rigid, I just stare at her profile. She's probably not speaking about the fun in the hay.

"I know you've kissed other girls before. But I haven't yet with a guy." Her long, dark lashes brush the skin beneath her eyes as she blinks. "My first kiss should be perfect. And real. One of true love. With the right man."

Behind her, my fingers curl into a fist. My voice gone flat from resentment, I conclude, "And *that* can only be a prince."

Her shy look meets mine. "Of course."

I lower my arm and hold my mug with both hands again. Lips compressed, I nod and draw in a deep breath as I glare into the hot chocolate. "Of course…"

How could I think for even a moment that things might be different? That just the smallest thing had changed between us? She's on a naïve mission to find her fair prince, who'll spring her free of our story. Maybe she's even right. No book of fairy tales has ever told the love story of a sweet girl and the big, bad Wolf.

A long moment passes in silence, as both of us seem lost in our thoughts. The stillness intensifies the patter of the heavy raindrops on the roof, and the trails of water on the windowpane blur the darkness outside. As if the sky had cracked open to wash away all my hopes that rose over the past two days.

Riley suddenly leans her head on my shoulder and startles me out of my musings. Eyes narrowed in suspicion, I slide a glance to her. She still looks into the flames, holding her drink tightly against her angled legs. "I wish you'd come to the ball tomorrow," she quietly says. "I might need a friend there."

I swallow. "All your friends will be there. You don't need me."

"But I *want* you there, too."

When Riley cuddles closer to me, tipping her knees to my side, I stiffen. Five minutes ago, she told me I couldn't kiss her. Now, she wants to creep under my skin? Her vision of the ideal ever after obviously includes the whole package. Adventure, a new ending, a lover…and me on top.

She wants it all, while I'm going to lose everything.

"You don't know what you're asking, honeydrop," I rasp with my eyes squeezed shut.

"I'm asking you to not give up on me." She sounds so sad when she says it. I know she values our new, deeper friendship just as much as I do. Only, in her heart, there isn't room for more. Not unless I spontaneously turn into a prince—which is fairly unlikely.

"I would never." I take the mug out of her hands, put it aside on the floor with mine, and finally lay an arm around her shoulders. Even without romance in our tale, she's been the center of my existence for as long as I can remember. Nothing will ever change that.

In spite of the heat from the fire, Riley shivers against me. I pull her closer and tenderly rub her upper arm for several silent minutes. With her head nestled under my chin, her breathing slows, becoming quiet and even.

She sounds on the verge of sleep as she murmurs, "You know what's funny, Jack?"

Gently, I stroke a wisp of hair behind her ear. "What?"

Her shy hand crawls up my chest, her fingers burying in my shirt. "You don't smell of wet dog at all."

I smile into the fire. "And you smell amazing…"

A few more seconds tick by, and then her voice sounds even fainter. "Please let me find you a happily ever after, too."

My chest lifts with a sigh. Holding her tightly, I don't give her an answer. Honestly, I don't care how much she wants to hook me up with some random princess to shape my ending the way *she* deems perfect. Because I already found my princess this week. And she's perfect for me.

Strange how this realization stabs my heart. We've spent an endless time together day after day… Though now, when I'm about to lose her, I finally understand what she really means to me.

I don't want to be replaced. Not in her story and not by her side.

Her satiny locks tickle my cheek as I try to look down at her porcelain face. I blow them away and then do what I wanted to do from the moment we sat down together. I gently run my fingers through her hair.

She shifts a little and sighs peacefully, the sound sparking my smile. If only she could abandon this stupid idea of love only happening among royals, then we could be like this…every day…every evening after playing our parts in our tale.

Tilting my head back on the sofa, I study the wooden ceiling with only the quiet crackling of the fire and her steady breathing for company now. There must be ten thousand knot-holes in the timber. One for each time we played together, I'm sure.

I refuse to believe that all of this could be over. Let's be frank, the chances of there being a prince sleeping in her trap come morning are slim to none. If I thought otherwise, I wouldn't have helped her build it in the first place. But Phillip's ball is tomorrow night. Blue-blooded guys from all corners of Fairyland will be there. They will dance with Riley and soon notice what a rare beauty she is. If she finds her new ever after in Phil's palace, nothing will ever be the same again.

Shifting my mouth thoughtfully to one side, I lift my head and study her face. She's asleep. I could carry her down to the cellar and lock her up until the ball is over.

Yeah, great idea, Jack. She'll totally be in love with you after that.

Or, I could just ask Phillip to cancel the party. No ball, no prince. But I don't want to get my friend into trouble with his wife. And knowing Riley, that wouldn't stop her from trying to find her destined majesty somewhere else, anyway. She might play cowgirl and go after the next one with a lasso.

Praise must be given to her creativity, though. I chuckle softly just thinking about her harebrained ideas so far. Heck, she even tried to kiss a *frog* into a prince! Crazy, or desperate? I close my eyes. Feisty…that's for sure. And something I've come to love most about this girl.

After following through with her plans the entire week, there's obviously only one way to win Riley's heart. I will have to snap myself into a prince, after all.

Unfortunately, there's no serum in Fairyland that can turn red blood blue. Dr. Jekyll won't be much help there. And all the witch spells in this damn place only work the other way round. I certainly don't need someone to permanently turn me into a swan, a frog, or a beast.

There you have it, Jack. No chance at all.

Unless…

Chapter 13

Riley

"Mmmmh," I moan, my fingers buried in soft, thick fur, and my face nestled against it as I return from the land of dreams back into my house. Jack was a man when we settled down together in front of the stove yesterday. Did he change into the Wolf overnight?

Slowly, my eyes flutter open. Bright morning light shines in on me from the east window of my hut, making me sneeze in greeting. My jerk doesn't rouse Jack. Apparently, the Wolf is a sound sleeper.

"Wake up, puppy dog," I mumble and shake the ball

of fur. He feels strange beneath my fingers, far too stiff. And flat. Did I squash him by lying on top of him? Sitting up, I rub the daze of sleep from my eyes and look down at Jack—who isn't Jack at all!

It's a grizzly bear skin, the one in front of my couch. Startled, I scan my cabin. It's empty. Jack is gone. Only the crackling fire keeps me company. He must have thrown a couple of logs into the stove before leaving. My long red cloak is draped over me, too, keeping me warm. It slides from my shoulders as I get up. No wonder I slept so well, tucked in like a baby bear.

Our two mugs from last night are still on the floor. I carry them over to the sink and open the kitchen window. Rain has gathered in the corner of the frame, pooling on the counter as I slide the pane. I wipe it away with a dishcloth and then poke my head out, calling, "Jack? Are you out there?"

The only answer is the merry chirping of my robin as he flutters down from the nest under the roof and settles on the windowsill. He fluffs up his feathers until he looks like a tiny ball of wool before he quickly shakes himself back into his petite form. There's always a small sack of birdseed in my cupboard. I fetch a few grains and hold them out in my palm. It tickles when the small beak picks them up, one by one.

"Have you seen my friend this morning?" I ask in a soft voice, not wanting to disturb the little bird's meal. "Tall man, dark hair, eyes like a wolf."

After he's done with his breakfast, the robin angles his strawberry-sized head from one side to the other, inspecting me with a beady eye in turn. Then he picks a couple of mites from his feathers, spreads his small, beautiful wings, and flies off.

"Great," I call after him, frowning. "Next time *you're* up to twaddling, don't expect me to be chatty."

Snorting, I turn back to the room, and my gaze alights on a piece of paper lying on the kitchen table. The brawny handwriting beckons me closer. My black pen lies next to the note. Jack must have gone on a raid through the chests to find it and the pad before he left.

The note in my hand, I sit down on a chair and read the few lines.

Dear Riley,

I need to run an errand outside town, which can't wait. I'll be back in a few days. You'll have to tell me everything about the ball then.
Good luck with the prince hunt!
Jack

P.S. Sorry for not waking you, but you looked extremely adorable drooling on the bear skin.

Quickly, I wipe the corner of my mouth with the back of my hand. Heck, I know I drool in my sleep at times. And he saw that? Heat sears my cheeks. Ugh. I want to drop into the hole to Wonderland again.

But what kind of errand is Jack talking about? And why didn't he mention anything yesterday? Stealing away in the dead of night is strange to the last E. Then again…didn't he say something about keeping Friday free for an adventure when we sat together by the lake the other day? Maybe it isn't an excuse, after all.

I put the note and pen away in the same drawer Jack took them from. After washing up quickly in the bathroom, I collect my cloak from the floor and fasten it around my neck. It's a shame that Jack is gone. I really wanted him to come with me to Rory and Phillip's masked ball tonight. Nevertheless, something else conjures a wide grin on my face this morning.

I've got a trap to check.

My escort to the ball might already be waiting there. Flittering out of the cabin, I slam the door shut and take off in a run along the path to the mill, my cloak flapping after me. Before the last bend, I halt and lean against a tree, catching my breath. If someone is lying in the prince bed, I don't want them to see me sweaty and panting.

First impressions are everything, right?

When the faint sounds of snoring drift to me, my muscles tense with excitement. I jerk up my head and hold my breath. Is there really someone sleeping in my trap? With Jack's disregard of my idea with the strawberries, I almost lost faith myself. But heck, here are the noises to prove my ingenuity.

Excitement is killing me as I tiptoe into the bushes where I tied the rope to a root last night. One quick pull, and the prince should be mine. Hopefully, he's a cutie-pie. My heart skips wildly in my chest as my fingers close firmly around the rope. I tighten it, ready to snap the trap shut. But then the raucous snoring makes me hesitate. Goodness, did he swallow a chainsaw?

With a man like this beside me in bed, I'm not sure I'll ever close an eye again for the rest of my life. Silently, I crawl closer to the bushes to peek at my trap. There isn't much to see, just a rolled-up bundle of a man on the pillow nest with his back to me. Hm. I bite the inside of my cheek. Maybe a closer look before pulling the stick away? It can't hurt.

Rising with the rope's end in my hand, I shake my hair back, straighten my spine, and nobly walk into the small clearing by the Timeless Brook with my head held high—just in case the man wakes up and sees me. At another strident snore, I wince. Oh, man…

I rub my hands over my face. *Get a grip, Riley. There's a crack in everything, and sleep is overrated anyway.* Also, there are many pros to staying awake forever. I can read all the books from the library in his surely amazing palace, for instance. Or binge-watch every cool show I've missed out on because I have no television in the woods.

With new courage in my heart, I draw closer, quietly bending over the sleeping prince to catch a glimpse of his face. And freeze.

"Oh, no! No freaking way!" Grabbing one end of the blanket, I shake it so hard, the dwarf dozing in the trap flies off in a high arch. "You…! Get out of my prince bed!"

Sleepy jerks awake as he lands on his behind and stares at me with stunned, saucer-like eyes. He takes his pointed brown hat off and scratches his shaggy white hair. "Red Riding Hood? What are you doing behind the Seven Hills?" He finishes the last word with a mighty yawn.

"This is not behind the Seven Hills, you bumbler. You took a nap in my trap." My gaze gets stuck on some red sauce in the corner of his mouth. "And you ate all the berry bait!"

"Oh, that was your bed?" Hands braced on the ground, he pushes himself to his feet, butt rising first. "I thought it was a rain shelter for hungry dwarfs."

What? I narrow my eyes at him. "Who would ever build such an odd thing?"

Sleepy shrugs.

"A prince might have come by last night, and now he's gone forever because you blocked the bed." Growling in frustration, I turn around and trudge off into the bushes. Someone needs to go on trap watch again. Only, my foot gets tangled in the rope, and it tightens as I stumble, trying to catch my balance. The stick is pulled free from the ground, and the trap snaps shut over the empty pillow-nest, coming down in a clattering rumble. All the laths fall apart, leaving nothing but a giant pile of wood behind.

Terrific.

My chin drops to my chest, and I stare at the ruins of my wonderful plan. Without Jack's help, there's no chance of repairing this, and the Blue Fairy only knows how long he'll be gone.

Something pulls at my cloak. The white-bearded dwarf next to me holds up his hand as I tilt my head to look down at him. A single strawberry lies on his palm. His bushy eyebrows lift in a sad look, and Sleepy snuffles, "I'm sorry, Miss Riley."

Expelling a sigh, I sit down beside him, take the fruit from his hand, and stuff it into my mouth.

*

In the early evening, the failure of plan T for trap is long forgotten. Back to plan B. The ball. After returning all the pillows and blankets to my house, a hot bath with rosy bubbles is on the list. Clean and smelling nice, I put on my finest red silk underwear. Something special will go on top tonight. There's a chest beneath my bed, holding the treasure of a beautiful velvet gown. My mother's old wedding dress.

A snicker of excitement escapes me as I step into it. Unfortunately, getting the zipper up in the back is a bit of a challenge. I skip through the room, struggling with it until it's finally fastened and I can look at myself in the mirror. Dark red velvet hugs my breasts, long sleeves of white voile cover my arms and hands. Under my chest, the skirt flows down to part over white silk in the front. The hem touches my ankles. It's truly lovely. The only thing that looks slightly out of place is my leather half boots, but they're better than appearing at the ball barefoot.

Squealing in anticipation of tonight, I twirl around, holding my arms up in the position of having a handsome dance partner. I smile at the air where his head would be. Oh, he'd surely have a beautiful face. Blue eyes. Sweet lips. A slim crown perched on his hair... Dancing ever so lightly around the room, I sway my head and start singing.

"I know you, I walked with you once upon a dream..."

The smell of something burning makes me stop two seconds later. Where the heck is that coming from? Rooted to the spot, I scan the area around me. Odd, there's nothing on the stove, and the fire's banked, yet the smell is unmistakable. When a strange heat licks up my legs, I angle my head and look down.

"Oh, my *Goodness*!" My mother's gown is on fire! I leap backward in reflex to escape the sneaky flames but, of course, the dress comes along. "Crud!" Hysterically patting at the sizzling fabric, I jump around in the room until I stumble out onto the porch. Puddles from last night's rain still litter the forest in many places. Without thinking, I dive into one, belly-flopping on the squelchy ground.

The cool water and mud assure me that I'm not going up in flames like a freaking match. Catching my breath, I sit up and examine the dress. Yep, the fire is extinguished. Sadly, so are my plans for tonight.

Half of my mother's velvet gown is charred, the rest of it is stained with mud. The hem must have brushed an ember and started the terrible destruction. Going like this, I would be the swineherd at the masked ball. Tears spring to my eyes.

Dabbing at my cheeks and thereby smearing sludge from my fingers all over my skin, I scramble to my feet and shuffle back to the three stairs leading up my porch. Since the dress is ruined beyond repair, it doesn't matter that the rags hang into another puddle as I sit down.

Elbows braced on my thighs, I bury my face in my hands. Now I'll never find a prince or a happily ever after for myself.

Jack will be so gleeful. He'd thought it was crap all along. I can just imagine his taunting sneer when he comes back saying, "Told you so."

With every breath, my heart hurts more.

As if feeling my grief, my little robin friend glides to my side and plops down on his behind, stretching his fragile legs in front of him, the claws pointing up into the air. Wings hanging, he tilts his head up to me and gives a pathetic chirp.

Seriously, I don't know which of us looks more miserable at the moment. The weeping bird, or the muddy-faced scarecrow in the burned rags. The thought almost coaxes a smile from me.

Carefully, like touching a butterfly, I brush my fingertips over the robin's back. "There, there... Don't look so sad. Some things just aren't meant to be, are they?"

He opens his beak to let out another sad chirp then rubs his head against my hand, wiping away a tiny bird tear. With a deep sigh, I rise and walk inside, taking my little friend with me. I put him in his favorite spot on the open window ledge before trudging into the bathroom. Time to clean up the mess I made.

As I come back a while later, clad in my simple red dress again with a white blouse beneath it, Alice's clock on the chest shows a quarter to five. That means it's past eight already. The ball has begun. Since my friends arranged the feast not only for Phillip's birthday but also for me, I should let them know I won't make it.

Barefoot, I traipse outside and lift my face to the purple evening sky. In the dimming light, sporadic storks zoom through the colorful streaks of clouds. Like before, I raise an arm and tap my fingers twice to hopefully call down an envoy. Within seconds, a tall, black-and-white-feathered bird lands in front of me, adjusting his blue vest. "Good evening. What can I do for you?"

I can't message them all. Since Princess Cinderella always arrives late to celebrations, it's probably best to pick her as the recipient. She can pass on the news to the others when she gets there. Clasping my hands in front of my stomach, I clear my throat.

"This is a message from Riley Redcoat to Princess Cinderella." A pause should mark the real text. "My dress caught on fire. I can't come to the ball tonight. Have fun with the girls and wish Phillip happy birthday for me. Riley.”

With a nod, I finish my speech, and the SMS takes off into the sky. Melancholy eats at me as I watch him fly until he's long out of sight. My feet are getting cold in the grass. It's probably wise to go inside before I catch a cold, but a rising round of robins keeps me rooted. First, the ten or so birds fly in wild arcs, which is unusual at twilight. However, they soon form a solid ring. A chill runs down my spine.

If robins fly in circles, it means one thing. Magic is in the air.

On the horizon, a dot appears inside the dancing ring. I squint to make out what it is, which is impossible. It looks like a birthmark in the sky.

As the robins continue their circles of flight, the dot grows bigger, and a strange noise sets in. The sound is high-pitched like a rocket, but far away. It gets louder, deeper, and the spot grows to a white… Heck, is that a speed stork?

Perhaps Cindy's already sent me a message—a flash telegram that's obviously going to detonate on my porch! I duck my head, shrieking, as the thing races past me and knocks into the potted plant next to the door. The clay pot explodes in a loud clatter of shards.

Carefully, I take my hands down and turn around. An interesting woman lies sprawled in the mess, legs jammed up against the wall. My mouth drops open in silent shock.

A painful moan drifts from the jumble on the floor. "Dear me…" Then a pair of starlight blue eyes beams at me from upside down. She waves. "Hello there."

Wariness tenses my muscles. Cautiously, I draw closer, pitching up my eyebrows. "You battered my ficus…"

"Ah, sorry." She climbs to her feet and brushes leaves and dirt off her bottom. "That definitely wasn't one of my best landings."

Judging from the chaos on my porch, someone had better take away her flying license. There's no telling what else she's been battering. Halting on the top stair, I cock my head and throw her a sideways glance. "Who are you?"

Her face lights up. "Why, I'm the Fairy Godmother, my dear!"

Thick strands of her white hair are wound around pin curlers, a purple bathrobe covers her body, and her feet are stuck in yellow crocs. "You don't look like the Fairy Godmother."

She glances down at herself, and a snicker makes her curlers wobble. "Oh. Yes. That's because Cindy's message caught me at the spa. Pinocchio was just giving my back a massage." Her lids flutter shut as she expels a dreamy moan. "Those wooden hands work magic, trust me." In the next moment, her eyes shoot open again. With the little stick in her hand, she taps herself on the head and—*poof!*— the crocs and curlers are gone. Stars zap around her, brightening up my porch, as the bathrobe turns into an ostentatious, shiny white gown with gold embroidery around her voluptuous waist.

Startled, I trip back, knocking over the second ficus beside the door.

"Mmm, tsk tsk tsk," she mutters, slapping the wand into her palm as her brows knit with a skeptical frown. "A little clumsy, aren't you? Cindy said that you burned your dress. Now I can see how that might have happened."

Excuse me? *She* was the one who bolted into plant number one. Quickly, I get back to my feet. "Cindy talked to you about me?"

"Yes, my dear. Of course. Why else do you think I'm here?"

I actually have no idea.

She takes my hand and drags me into the house, chattering away. "Tonight is the grand masked ball at Aurora and Phillip's castle, is it not? Princess Cinderella told me it was the girls' idea to bring you a fine selection of princes." As she looks around my small home, she scratches her head with the pointed wand. "What you want with them all, I don't quite understand. Isn't one prince adequate for you?"

"One is definitely enough," I answer fast and nod vigorously. "I just didn't know where to find one, so they thought the ball might be a good place to start."

"Oh, right." Another smile sugars up her face. "And why did you set your dress on fire tonight, my dear?"

My gaze slides to the embers in the stove. "Er..." I work my lip between my teeth.

The fairy tracks my glance. "Hmm. You didn't try to use them as transportation, did you?" Her puzzled frown meets mine but eases just as fast. "No. You didn't."

I squeeze my eyes tight. "No, I didn't for sure."

"Good. Because it doesn't work in our world." She leans in close and whispers with a hand at the corner of her mouth. "I've tried."

The lady is nuts.

Something behind me catches her attention next. She whizzes past me and grabs the clock from Alice. "Oh, isn't this lovely?" With her index finger, she moves the minute hand around two circles, and the thing goes off with three grandfather clock-like chimes all of a sudden. "Well, it's late." Putting it back, she claps her hands. "Let's get to work."

Like a ficus in my own house, I stand rooted and just follow her strides with my wary eyes. "What are we going to do?"

"Oh, didn't I say?" Using her wand, she lifts my chin and beams at me. "Cindy sent me to your rescue. We're to give you a new dress." Then she cocks her head. "If you still want to go to the ball, that is."

A dress? The ball? Gripped by a bolt of excitement, I grab her hand holding the wand with both of mine. "I do!"

"Careful, dear child." She works her wand free of my grip. "We don't want this to go off by accident and turn you into a naked-ass baboon."

Goodness, no! We definitely don't want that. Keeping

my hands to myself, I start rocking on the balls of my feet. "What do I have to do?"

She takes a step back, still smiling. "Undress, darling." Next, she starts to fiddle her wand like a conductor's baton and, in a shower of stars, the enchanting light-blue ball gown from Cindy's personal fairy tale appears on an invisible hanger in the middle of the room. "And then slip into this."

Oh, holy Christmas tree! I clap my hands over my mouth, simply overwhelmed. "It's beautiful."

The glass slippers materialize beneath it on the floor. "Go, put it on," she prods me, waving her hands to usher me forward.

I strip as fast as I can, carelessly tossing my clothes aside. My blouse lands on the chest and knocks a photograph of Belle and me to the floor. In my underwear, I rush over and pick it up. Whoops. The glass frame shattered into a mosaic of a thousand cracks.

The fairy casts me a look of reprobation. Sheepishly, I grin back and return the frame to the shelf.

"Come over here, child, before you damage the entire house in your flurry." She holds the dress out to me so I can step into it. When she tugs it up and ties the laces in the back, sparkles suddenly whizz around the wide, bell-like bottom. They change the material to a deep rose red. In wonder, I watch the glowing stars spiral up around me. As if a paint pot was tipped over the dress, the new color seeps up along the fabric, getting fainter toward the waist and finally coloring the bodice a soft hue of pink.

As the sparkles move down my arms, the long, sheer sleeves of Cindy's dress disappear. A pair of elbow-length satin gloves replaces them, dyed in the same morning-sky pink. Stretching my arms out in front of me, I run my hand up the smooth fabric. My mouth is open all the while.

"Whoops. This is new," the fairy chimes out, giggling as she steps in front of me and inspects me from head to toe. "But it suits you well, I have to say."

I dash to the corner of the cabin that is my bedroom and open the door of the wardrobe with the tall mirror attached to the inside. In front of it, I twirl left and right, making the gorgeous, multi-layered, rosy gown swing and sway like a snowdrop in the winter breeze.

"Even though you seem to have personalized the dress, don't forget that it comes with a handicap, my dear."

The fairy appears behind me in the mirror, but I can't pay her any attention. Carefully, I run my hands over the little diamonds worked into the bodice that fade as they run down the gown. The light reflects off them like a sea of stars.

"At the twelfth strike of midnight, the gown and accessories will return to the magical closet of artifacts again."

The sleeves of the dress are now two simple, rosy voile bands that run around my upper arms. They keep my neck and shoulders bare.

"So you must leave the ball before midnight."

I can't breathe, steamrolled by so much beauty. It really is a miracle.

"Are you even listening?" The fairy bops me on the head with her wand. "This is important, girl."

"Ow!" Torn out of my admiration, I zap around, rubbing the sore spot on my crown. "Why did you do that?"

Her strict look bores into me. "Because you need to remember the rules. It would be disastrous to stay at the ball too long."

My eyes roll behind closed lids. "Okay, okaaay…" No need to whack out. "I don't intend to crash at the castle."

I lift my skirt, about to slip a naked foot into one of the beautiful glass shoes, but the lady slaps her wand on my chest and shoves me backward. "Uh, uh, uh!" Quickly, she bends and picks them up, protecting them against her décolleté as her gaze slides to the broken glass frame on the chest. "We'd better not give you those."

"No?" My face falls, voice weak from disappointment. "You want me to go to the ball barefoot?"

"Hmm." Scratching her chin, she drops the shoes.

I scream in terror, uselessly reaching out. But the slippers vaporize into thin air before they hit the ground. Rubbing my hands over my face, I expel a breath. Oh, man…

"There's only one other pair of shoes I have access to. They might not be as dreamy and elegant as the glass slippers"—she swishes her wand, pointing it at my feet, and her mouth curves like a banana—"but at least they're the right color."

Pulling up the skirt, I bend forward and look at my new footwear. Glittery red and wonderfully comfortable. I know these ruby slippers. Enthralled, I lift one foot and roll my ankle, marveling like a child in a candy shop.

The fairy giggles. "There's no chance you'll break *them*." In the next moment, concern swamps her face, and she shapes her palms to my cheeks, staring insistently into my eyes. "But whatever you do, don't click your heels together."

Swallowing, I give a firm nod. I don't want to be swept off to Kansas tonight.

"Now, there's only one thing left to do." She takes my hand and drags me out the door, throwing me a wry glance on the way. "You wouldn't happen to be friends with some mice, would you?"

If she's thinking about changing some rodents into fine horses and harnessing them to a pumpkin, sadly, she'll be disappointed. "Sorry, no."

"Ah, no worries, my dear. We'll find something else for you." Pulling the door closed behind us, she scans the porch. Goodness, I hope she's not on the lookout for any roaches. That would be gross.

Her gaze lifts to the nest under the roof from where my tiny friend watches us curiously. "Hey, you there," she calls, pointing her wand at the robin, and her face brightens with delight. "Come down, my lovely, would you?" As she holds out her hand, the tiny bird glides into it and moves his gaze back and forth between us. "A little tap of this, and a little swirl of that..." the Fairy Godmother sings as she waves her wand around the robin. In the next moment, the little fella grows and grows and grows—until it doesn't fit under my awning anymore.

The brown coat has changed into white fur, four hooves have replaced the delicate claws, and when it shakes its head, a silky mane wafts in the wind. The only thing that remains from the bird is the wings, but they, too, have grown substantially.

My chin smacks on my chest.

"Shoo, shoo! We don't want you late to the ball." The fairy pushes me gently with a hand on my back, assisting me as the beautiful winged stallion bends his front legs and lowers, allowing me to mount.

The only time I've ever sat on a horse was with Phillip a few days ago. My knees tremble, and my hands start to sweat. Holy Pegasus, let's hope I survive the ride.

"Oh, wait!" Madam Fairy pulls on the elegant reins, keeping the horse back for another moment. "I almost forgot..." Lifting her hand, she twirls one of my locks around the tip of her wand. Over the next three seconds, I can feel how my hair shapes up at the back of my head. Some loose strands hang down and brush my bare shoulders.

As something soft covers the top half of my face, I

reach up to feel around my eyes and nose. It's a satiny mask, and I would bet my cloak that it's the same color as the glamorous dress.

If only Jack could see me now. He wouldn't believe his eyes.

With a grateful smile, I lean down and squeeze the fairy's hand. "Thank you so much for everything."

"You're very welcome, my dear. And now…" As she steps behind the horse, a loud smack sounds. "Off you go!"

With a feral snicker, my changed robin friend gallops off, his mighty feathered wings beating the air. A hoarse cry escapes me. I grab the beast's mane in panic, holding on tightly as, three strides later, we're airborne and racing across the sky, heading for Castle Grove.

The wind blows in my face, forcing my eyes shut as fear of plummeting to death takes hold and gives me a chill. The flight is smooth, though, and soon, my dread eases. I even dare a look down.

Goodness, this is beautiful. The Wood of 1000 Dawns sweeps by under us, and there, in the distance, the stunning lights of Aurora's palace appear. We start a gentle descent, and the horse takes the final strides back on the ground, directly into the castle's pebbled front garden.

Like before, the beast bends its front legs to make it easy for me to get off. As soon as my feet touch solid ground, the mighty white stallion shrinks to bird size and pops back into my cute robin friend. With a happy chirp, he says goodbye before he takes off in the direction we came from. I guess that means a march home for me after the ball.

It doesn't matter since I usually come here by foot anyway. The two miles through the forest won't kill me, even after a night of dancing.

When the robin is out of sight, I turn around and stare at the huge, winged doors of the castle that are wide open tonight. Two guards stand watch on the left and right, holding their spears formally by their sides and gazing straight forward. I greet them both with a hesitant nod, my eyes moving shyly from one to the other. Hopefully, they don't expect the guests to show an official invitation because there's certainly none stored in this enchanted dress. But neither of them moves a muscle, diffusing my worries.

All right. Here we go. Lifting the front of my dress a few inches off the ground so I don't trip over the hem, I cross the threshold.

My ever after is waiting.

Chapter 14

Riley

Rory's castle is an impressive sight even on normal days. Tonight, it's a dream.

Big bows and intricate lanterns decorate the walls. They bear the colors of Phillip's family crest—white, blue, and silver. Hundreds of candles illuminate my way as I stroll through the high entry hall and move to the east wing. The path is flanked by countless pink and white rose petals, suffusing the air with a wonderful scent.

I've never walked into a truer fairy tale than this.

As if carried by golden clouds, I gravitate to the strains

of string music softly drifting to me. Another late couple flitters past me down the hallway. The woman's marvelous midnight-blue dress sweeps across the floor as the heels of her attendant's boots clack on the stone.

With a faint heart, I follow them and wonder if it'll look strange for me to appear alone. On the other hand, that's the whole point of me coming here, isn't it? If I'm attached to the arm of a gentleman, no foreign prince will even think about approaching me. Better to communicate that I'm single straightaway.

The sweet music gets louder, the chatter of people mingling with it. A few steps ahead, the hallway ends at the top of a wide stairwell that leads directly down into the grand ballroom I've only ever seen empty.

What might it be like tonight, filled with hundreds of people from all corners of Fairyland? Will I even fit in?

My nerves tie themselves into a tight bundle. Playing princess in my house in a dress that doesn't belong to me is one thing. But it's a totally different matter to wear it in a palace full of born-and-bred royals as if I actually own the gown. They'll out me as the girl from the woods straightaway. I'd better wait for a good moment when everyone is distracted and then quickly sneak downstairs.

My steps falter, and I grip the dark red floor-to-ceiling curtains that are drawn aside at the entrance. Frightfully hanging on to them, I struggle to rein in my erratic breathing. If only Jack was here to give me some courage now. Damn him for running out of town at the last minute. I start to wonder if it was an excuse, after all. Something he told me so he wouldn't have to show up at the ball tonight.

My heart pounds in my throat. Perhaps he should have taken me with him.

A fold of the thick curtain still clasped tightly in my fist for support, I dare a step forward and sneak a glance into the ballroom. All I can see on this level, however, is a giant chandelier hanging from the high ceiling in the center of the room. The thousand crystal drops beautifully reflect light beams in all shades of the rainbow.

"May I help you, milady?" a raspy voice makes me snap back to the protection of the curtains. My hand flies to my pounding heart.

The young man in front of me is dressed in some sort of white uniform with silver embroidery on the front of his jacket and his light blue banded collar. A rapier attached to his left hip hangs down his leather-clad leg, making him look a lot like the guards outside. But a silver mask covering the top half of his face implies that he's a guest in the castle, too.

A real prince. *Oh, my Goodness!* My eyes feel as if they've just gone glassy with panic.

It takes a moment for my voice to return. "Um…no, thank you. I was just—"

"Scared of walking down?"

Am I that easy to read? I should watch the feast from up here then.

"Yeah. Maybe a little." Admitting it out loud actually eases some of my tremors, and I can breathe again. "It's my first ball of this kind."

He cocks his head in amusement, clasping his hands behind his back. "The *masked* kind?"

The *kind* where I pretend to be a princess and find a lover. But it's probably better not to say *that* aloud. I just nod.

"You shouldn't be scared." His lips curve into a gentle smile. "You look amazing."

The unexpected compliment brings a warm blush to my cheeks. I lower my face, squinting up at him through my lashes. "Thank you."

Behind the mask, he blinks his incredibly blue eyes. They stand out in stark contrast to his white-powdered hair. "Would you like me to escort you down?"

I grimace. The heavy curtains at my back feel far safer than walking off with this royal right now. "That's very kind of you. But I'm afraid I need another minute."

He looks at me as if considering whether I want him to wait. In the end, he seems to understand that I'd rather be alone.

"Very well." The young man nods politely, yet his intense gaze lingers another second. A gossamer tickle runs over the skin of my neck. "I hope I'm fortunate enough to catch a dance with you later."

I swallow. When words obviously fail me, his lips twitch into a one-sided smile. He heads off into the ballroom, sliding a last glance in my direction before he disappears down the stairs.

My heart pounds like a kettledrum, wanting to follow him. But my feet grow roots into the stone floor. After he's gone, I bite my lip and turn around to giggle into the curtains. What an enjoyable encounter. If I can go by this start, the night might turn out lovely, after all.

"Oh, there you are!"

With a little jump, I whirl back and find Snow-White and Belle flitting toward me from the stairs. "We've been looking for you everywhere," Belle chimes out as they stop in front of me, each clasping one of my hands. The slim mask the Beauty wears over her eyes that matches her dress doesn't conceal her identity. I just knew she wouldn't be able to resist wearing purple tonight. "What are you doing up here? The feast is downstairs! You're going to miss everything."

Panicking, I back into the curtains again. "I was…getting prepared."

Her fists propped on the waist of her silver gown with lots and lots of black spots, Snow-White casts me a take-no-shit look. The cat ears headband she wears and the small, black kitty nose concealing her own, along with whiskers drawn across her cheeks, dash the grim expression a little. "Well then, I hope you're ready because you're coming with us." She tugs at my hand. Because there are two of them—and Belle is actually a lot stronger than her fragile stature implies—I don't stand a chance.

Every step that brings me nearer to the light shining out from the ballroom makes my heart pound faster. I try to concentrate on the rainbow beams from the chandelier to calm myself, but totally lose the battle when we reach the landing, and my friends mercilessly drag me downstairs.

My gaze sweeps across the hall, and my breath hitches.

The room that is usually so cold and bare has been transformed into a real spring fairy tale tonight. Tendrils of pink roses wind up each of the twelve floor-to-ceiling marble columns around the room. Countless tables covered with platters of dreamy tarts, cakes, cupcakes, and bowls of pudding line the walls between them. On the pedestal near where the string quartet belts out a lovely song, a pyramid of champagne glasses, all filled with bubbly golden liquid, sits. Every so often, a passing guest takes one away from the top.

In the center of the room, a two-inch glass platform covers the diamond-shaped pool built into the stone surface that is obviously the dance floor. Even from where I stand, I can make out the countless goldfish weaving gracefully through the crystal-clear water. The space is still empty, the colorful sea of people moving around it as they chatter and laugh.

Pulled into the dreamy ambiance of the place, I stop dead halfway down the stairwell—and cause Belle to slip and land on her bottom.

"Oh. I'm so sorry!" I rush the two steps down and help

her up. "Are you all right?"

She rolls her eyes but laughs. "Fortunately, I already had my grand entrance with Dominic when we got here." Getting to her feet, she rubs her behind. "Would have been quite the gossip tonight if this was how I arrived."

Snow-White snickers. "It'll make for some good gossip anyway."

I track her gaze back to the feast and find three hundred pairs of eyes fixed on us. My cheeks grow so hot, I'm sure I'm raising the temperature in the room by several degrees—and it wasn't even me that landed on my butt.

So much for sneaking in.

Head lowered and gaze focused on the stairs—making sure I don't miss a step—I let the girls pull me all the way down, much slower than before. Relief washes over me when we make it to the bottom without another embarrassing incident, and I finally can hide in the crowd.

I don't know where my friends are going and blindly follow, totally getting disoriented among so many people. Women have come in gorgeous gowns wearing masks as simple as mine and some without. A few wear masks shaped into animal faces or powdered wigs. Most men are clad in fine linen shirts and uniform jackets, revealing a hint of vest. White-haired wigs seem to be the norm, even among the male visitors. I guess this is the royal manner of dress when going to a ball.

I hurry after Snow-White and Belle, struggling not to lose them in the chaos of people. Heck, where are they running to so fast? "Snowy!" I call out in panic as her silver and black dress flitters in and out of sight. But I don't know if she even heard me because a bird suddenly stops my chase. Not a real bird, of course, but a young man in the disguise of a beautiful robin—one I totally knock into.

Where the hell did he flutter in from? He cups my elbows and balances me as I trip in Dorothy's shoes. As I catch my breath, a hand to my chest, I look up. He wears a mask that is speckled with a myriad of multihued feathers, covering most of his face down to the sensual curve of his lips. From between two slits, dark eyes sparkle in the crystal light of the chandelier above us.

"Are you all right?" he drawls ever so slowly, making me forget the fast-moving world around us. It strangely makes my heart calm down.

"Mm-hmm." I nod, my attention drawn to his dark hair with the lighter streaks of feathers worked into it. They match the color of his feathered cape. A deep orange linen shirt creates an enchanting contrast, marking my favorite animal. A truly beautiful masquerade.

I should apologize for nearly knocking him to the floor, but what actually issues past my lips shocks me. "I love robins."

A long moment passes as he just looks at me. His fingers on my elbows start gliding down my forearms to my hands. He holds them gently and tilts his head. Beneath the small obtrusion that forms his beak, a small smile appears. "Do you?"

"Riley!" Snow-White's upset voice cuts between us. "How did you get lost again? Hurry up now, everyone's waiting." She loops her hand around my upper arm and pulls me away, casting the robin an apologetic look that makes her cat nose wrinkle.

When Belle pops up behind her and nabs my other arm, there's no escaping the demand of my friends.

"Sorry, I have to go." A regretful frown creasing my brow, I hope he can read how much I'd rather stay and talk about my favorite birds.

He nods, the smile still hidden in the secret place beneath his mask as the girls pull me away. "I hope to see you again…Riley."

Dear me, I hope that, too.

Giggling, I hurry off with Snow-White and Belle, who don't let go of my arms again. Prince Dominic shocks me as he suddenly rushes at us from the side, sweeping his girlfriend away into a worried embrace. "Did you hurt yourself on the stairs, darling?" he demands, skimming a few loose curls free from her forehead.

"I'm fine," she assures him with a smile. He doesn't let go of her again. They follow us as Snow-White pulls me toward the cupcake table set up between two columns and finally slows down. But I don't get a second to catch my breath because Princess Cinderella storms over to us, clad in a beautiful sunset-orange dress with long gloves. From the speed with which she comes at me, I know she's going to crush me in an embrace.

"Girl! What took you so long?" she blares into my ear, knocking the air out of my lungs. "Did the Fairy Godmother find you? We feared she missed your house!" Then she holds me away from herself, hands tight on my shoulders. "Goodness!" Her eyes nearly pop out. "You're beautiful! Is that my dress? It doesn't look like it."

I don't know which of her questions to answer first. "Umm…"

"You have to tell me everything, in detail…later." Her face splits into a grin. "Now, we have a surprise for you."

"Oh. Really?" What could that be? A new arrow from Cupid's tree so I can shoot someone with it tonight?

"Ta-da!" Cindy steps aside, proudly presenting a cheerful Aurora balancing on crutches in a fitted turquoise dress that opens on one side. The slit in the glittery fabric frees her right leg, which is entirely wrapped in a cast.

My smile falls in shock. "Something's clearly wrong with your humor, Cindy."

"No, honey, you don't understand." Radiating excitement, she draws up beside me, drapes an arm around my shoulders, and holds me tightly against her as she cheers next to my face, "It means you'll get a very special honor tonight."

I narrow my eyes at her. "What honor? To be the first to sign Rory's cast?" Still baffled, I carefully hug the invalid princess. "What in the world did you do to yourself?"

"I thought it would be fun to throw myself over a root in the garden last night." Aurora laughs as she sits down on an upholstered chair. Someone must have brought it in especially for her because I don't see any other chairs around.

Her type of entertainment is not amusing. It's terrible that she has to sit out her own ball. "I can imagine things way more fun than that."

"Oh, don't worry." She waves a dismissive hand. "It's not that bad. It'll heal."

After weeks, yeah. I know how long it took my broken wrist to heal. Wait until the itching begins. An entire leg…*ugh*. A shudder rakes over me at the thought.

I turn to Cindy and Snow-White. "So, what is the honor you spoke of?"

No one answers, their attention caught by a man in a dark cloak, hood drawn over his head, and one side of his face covered by a white mask. Only when he hands Aurora a glass of champagne and kisses her on the temple, do I recognize the phantom as Phillip.

"Riley!" The one visible half of his mouth curves as he notices me. Then his appreciative gaze moves down and up my dress for a moment. He whistles through his teeth. "Look at you."

Help! Another blush is on the rise. I grimace. "Yeah…it's actually not mine."

His eyes take on a humorous gleam as he leans in and whispers, "Are they ever?" Then he straightens again and turns an impish grin on Belle next to me. "Awesome slip on the stairs, by the way."

Laughing, she smacks him on the shoulder. "Shut up, you!"

He rubs the spot, certainly not in pain, but his attention skates back to me. "You had some people worried you wouldn't show up tonight."

I bet. "Getting dressed for a ball is harder than one might think." My comment holds a lot of truth, which surely reflects in my tone as I cast a glance at Cindy, silently saying thanks for the fairy miracle earlier. Then I remember the real reason for the feast and step up to Phillip, breathing a kiss on his cheek. "Happy birthday."

"Thank you." He lightly wraps his arm around my waist and smirks. "I hear I'm going to open the first waltz with you tonight."

"You are?" In shock, I lean back but can't escape him.

"Oh, yes," Cindy answers for him, and all my friends flash bright grins my way. "Surprise!"

A frightened little "huh?" escapes me.

"Someone has to stand in for me," Rory says, pointing at her broken leg. "Because, obviously, I can't dance."

"And that someone is me?" My voice trembles, as do my lips. Fortunately, Phillip is still holding me, or I'd probably keel over, what with my knees turning into pudding and all. "Why not Cindy? Or Snowy?"

"Because this is the perfect opportunity to show you off to the many dukes and princes here," Aurora explains, waving her hands excitedly in the air from her chair. "When they see you dancing, and in this awesome dress, they'll line up to dance with you."

"Speaking of, we better get moving," Phillip adds cheerfully, taking off the dark cloak and draping it over Rory's chair. "Everyone's already waiting." Like most of the men in here, he's wearing a uniform, the silver embroidery on the white fabric reminding me of the jacket the stranger upstairs wore. Only instead of a band collar, Phillip's has a lapel in a much darker blue—the same color as his uniform pants. "No couple is going to dance tonight before the host does." He pulls me away from the others, steering me across to the glass dance floor with the water underneath.

Anxious, I drag him to a halt as I carefully put one foot onto the glass, testing it first with half of my weight, then putting even more on it.

"It'll hold. Promise." He laughs but gives me a moment to adjust. "If eighty dancing couples can't break it, you surely won't."

My nervous gaze moves to him. Phillip encourages me with a smile and holds out his elbow for me to grab on to. He escorts me to the very center of the platform and lifts his hand to draw attention. Amazing how the entire room goes instantly quiet. Even the music stops.

"Good evening, ladies and gentlemen." His voice carries loud and clear through the hall. "And welcome to our ball."

Frightened, I look around because I still feel absolutely out of place, even attached to Phillip's arm. This is Rory's place, not mine. It's also her privilege to perform the first dance of the evening with the prince. They shouldn't have surprised me with this…nightmare.

"Because my sweet wife lost a fight with a root yesterday and broke her leg, the lovely Lady Riley has given me the honor of the first dance and will open the ball with me tonight." He tilts his head at me and whispers, "Ready?"

"Uh-uh," I utter with slight hysteria, eyes so wide that the light hurts as it seemingly tries to stab through to the back of my skull.

"You don't need to be afraid." Brushing off my panic with a warm smile, Phillip takes my hand in his and places the other at the small of my back. "Just follow my lead."

After his quick nod to the musicians, they strike the first sweet chords of an enchanting, slow song, and Phillip begins to move with me.

He takes very small steps at first as if testing whether I know how to dance. I've certainly learned enough from my princess friends in the past to suffice, but with my nerves still in a tight knot, I appreciate him giving me time to adjust. It's also quite a challenge to overcome the fear of falling through the glass and right into the water at every next step.

"Don't look down. It's easier that way."

Wow, Phillip is quite observant. Or maybe he just remembers how he felt his first time dancing on this floor. I follow his advice and concentrate on his eyes instead. He was right. Much easier.

I take the moment that we have to ourselves—even if we have three hundred witnesses gathered around the dance floor—to ask Phillip what's been on my mind. A subject I didn't want to bring up in front of my friends. "Do you know where Jack went?"

The prince nods. "He dropped by this morning and said something about going to meet someone outside of town. He should be back soon."

"Do you think perhaps it was an excuse so he didn't have to come here with me tonight?"

Phillip chuckles, cutting a glance at the ceiling. "Mmmmaybe…"

I knew it!

When the prince's gaze returns to me, it's sober. "But he also said to tell you that you look amazing…if you did." His face softens even more. "And you *do* look beautiful tonight."

"Thank you." This time, I don't blush at his compliment. I don't know what it is—the dress, the music, or perhaps because it really *is* an honor to get the first dance of a ball with the lord of the castle—but I feel my spine straighten all of a sudden. It's much easier to keep my chin up and a confident expression on my face. "Also for offering your birthday party to help me."

"Nah, don't worry about that. The annual cruises to Treasure Island became boring many years ago. This is a nice change for once. I really hope you're enjoying yourself here."

My mouth kicks up into a smile. "I'm starting to." It's the truth, I really ease up. Phillip seems to notice it, too, because he acknowledges it with an approving nod. At the next crescendo of the song, his steps suddenly stretch, and he sweeps me in amazing, wide twirls across the glass dance floor.

For one short moment, he takes his hand off my waist and waves an invitation for the guests to join us. Jassie and Aladdin, and Ariel and Prince Eric are the first to step onto the transparent floor. They nod at us in greeting before they waltz away. Soon, the place fills up fast with more couples, and we're swallowed by the crowd.

It's a miracle that with so many people on the glass floor, we don't knock into other dancers. Then again, it's probably because Phillip is the host of the feast, and they all keep a respectful distance. There's even enough space for him to twirl me away and pull me back into his arms. Head tilted back, I laugh out loud.

Holding me tightly, he looks into my eyes, a question lingering in his gaze. When he cocks an eyebrow, I know he's asking me if he can do it again. And I nod. The next moment, he gives my waist a slight push to twirl me away from him, our hands still joined over the distance. Only this time, his grip eases at the end of my swirl, and suddenly, I'm in the arms of someone else.

A gasp escapes me, my head jerking around as I'm swept away. My new partner falls so easily into the rhythm that I never even have to break stride. In an acute panic, I scan over his shoulder to find Phillip. The prince came to a halt where I left him alone in the crowd, eyes fixed on us. When our gazes meet across the space, he gives a helpless shrug…right before his lips twitch into a smirk.

Other couples cut into the space between us and block him from my view. Slightly out of breath from shock, I finally shift my gaze to the face of my captor—and find myself staring into incredibly blue eyes framed by a silver mask.

Chapter 15

In graceful circles, my new dance partner twirls us around and around and around. The stranger with the rapier easily weaves into the flow of the dancing crowd. Luckily, I know the steps of a waltz quite well and don't let panic freeze me. That would cause a funny pileup in the middle of the dance floor for sure. Nevertheless, I wish he would ease up on his firm grip and let me escape. Phillip made me feel utterly safe and protected when he steered me across the glass platform. But with the intense gaze of this blond noble man fastened on my eyes instead, I feel strangely like prey.

"What—in—who...?" My voice sounds like the croak of a dying frog. We make an entire lap around the dance floor before my tongue forms a coherent sentence. "Why did you steal me away?"

His haunting gaze has never left mine this entire time, and my question is met with a small smile as if he finally appreciates me speaking. "With over fifty gentlemen waiting to dance with you, I wanted to be the first."

"Well, you're hardly the first. The lord of the castle surprised me with the news of opening the ball with him three minutes ago." I make a wry face since the man seems to know nothing about etiquette. "He's actually the one you stole me from."

"There are plenty of other fine women to dance with." He waves a hand at the many people surrounding us. "The prince can have his choice. Besides, Phillip is my cousin. I'm sure he doesn't mind."

My breath freezes in my lungs as I stare into the gleaming sapphire orbs behind the silver mask. Phillip's eyes are blue, too, if not this striking. And they both have fair hair. My gaze quickly flows down his body and then rushes up again. Same build and similar uniforms. Holy dream castle, is it a stroke of fate that I'm dancing with a close relative of Rory's husband? She did say this week how lovely it would be for me to marry into their family.

Phillip's cousin leans so close that I can feel his lips moving as he drawls into my ear, "I bet now you're surprised."

With lowered lids, I try to hide the shiver that his warm breath on my skin just triggered. "Maybe…a little." Then my gaze snaps up to his face once more. "Shouldn't the *plenty of fine women* have worked for you, too? No need to rob your cousin of his dance partner."

"None of the others interest me like you do."

My eyebrows quirk in astonishment. "I…do?" And I'm back to stammering again. Dang it. This is not how a princess would behave. He'll debunk me as a phony in no time. Not only will he lose interest in me, but the rest of the single men at the feast will think that I'm a waste of time, too.

Pull yourself together, Red Riding Hood, and don't ruin this!

"I mean…that is very kind of you, Prince…"

"Jacob of the Snow Plains." He cracks a teasing smile. As if his name should ring a bell.

"Oh, the Snow Plains." They are legendary, even though I know nothing about the royal family who reigns there. "Aren't they far up in the Marble Mountains? It is said to be the most beautiful place in Fairyland's North."

"It certainly is." The string quartet ends their song, and we come to a halt with all the other couples on the glass deck. Still holding my hand, he bends forward and plants a gentle kiss on my knuckles. His brows move up as his gaze locks with mine. "But not as beautiful as you, Lady Riley."

My hand trembles under his lips. He may be a dance partner thief, but he certainly has the charm of a true prince.

"Would you honor me with another dance, milady?" he asks softly as he straightens again, smiling down at me.

I'm just about to nod when someone interrupts our lovely moment. "I daresay it's my turn to kidnap the fair princess for a dance."

The voice is faintly familiar—I've heard it before, I'm sure. However, it takes a look into a feathered mask for me to recognize who it is. The robin.

His striking orange linen shirt stands out against the dark leather pants and boots of his costume. He no longer wears the beautiful, feather-embroidered cape from earlier. If his intention is to dance, it makes sense. The precious thing would only be in the way.

I would love to sway across the dance floor with Jacob once more, yet the robin's request flatters me. When he holds out his hand to me, I instinctively put mine in it and send Jacob an apologetic smile. Except, he doesn't even see it. The two men appear to be fighting a silent staring battle, neither of them backing down an inch. As if the alphas of two wolf packs were standing in front of me. Their gazes are like fire and ice.

Perhaps it's best to leave the guys to themselves and return to my friends. I certainly didn't come to this ball to start any rivalries. With my hand already clasped by the bird man, however, there's no means of escape. And he makes sure of that by wrapping his fingers tighter around mine.

He's also the first one to break the stare between Jacob and him before he turns to look at me. His face lights up with a warm smile as he walks me a few steps backward, away from Prince Jacob. The new song is much softer than the one before, the waltz a few beats slower. In a perfect dance position, we begin to move. Only this time, we twirl on the spot instead of dancing around the entire glass deck.

"Are you enjoying the feast, Lady Riley?" He tilts his head to one side as if trying to read my face and my reaction to him disrupting my encounter with the Prince of the Snow Plains.

I love the tender accent on my name when he rolls the R. It feels like the single word is sliding all the way down my body. "I've barely had a minute to breathe. But the company is very nice. The only thing that worries me is that I keep getting abducted by strangers."

"Strangers?" He chuckles. "That is a rough term, don't you think?"

"Hardly. I don't even know your name."

"Let me tell you then." He swings me around in a zestful swirl in order to avoid a collision with an oncoming couple, and I feel how my gown fans out. When our dance is slower again, he gives me a dimpled smile. "I am Jaccomo Casanova. Prince of the South, and Duke of Secret Garden."

My chin almost drops. "That is an incredibly long

name." If I've even heard it before, no wonder I can't remember.

He laughs softly. "How about you just call me Jaccomo?"

Thank the thirteen fairies. That sounds a lot more manageable than the entire litany of his title.

Again, he moves me out of harm's way when Cindy and Jason sweep past. In a turn when Jaccomo can't see it, she flashes me a grin and gives me a thumbs-up over her husband's shoulder before they disappear into the crowd again.

"I should have known that no man in this room would give you up easily."

My attention is drawn back to my dancing partner. He looks like a robin, but his eyes are as sharp as those of a predator. I don't know if it's his intense gaze or his compliment that causes a light sizzle over my skin.

"Oh, now I think you're exaggerating."

"Am I?" He casts a brief glance to the side of the dance floor.

I turn my head, too, and find Prince Jacob still standing there. His right hand clasps the hilt of his sword, ready to draw, and a muscle works his jaw.

A soft laugh caresses my ear. "I bet he'd love to behead me for taking you away from him."

The tickle on my neck from his breath makes me lower my head, but my gaze lingers for another short moment on the ousted prince. Would he really? The knuckles of his hand turn white from his hard grip on the rapier's hilt. A wave of nervousness rolls through me, and I miss a step. "Goodness, he wouldn't really, would he? He's got a sword."

"Your worry about my safety honors me, dear Riley. But I can assure you, I know how to defend myself. It wouldn't be the first battle I've fought in my life."

"It sure would be the first battle that someone fought over *me*," I croak, barely able to rein in my drumming heart.

With frightened eyes, I search Jacob's face until he allows our gazes to lock again across the distance. Silently, I plead with him not to do anything reckless. Every second that he stares at me with narrowed eyes feels like hours. Eventually, the hard lines of his face soften. His hand slips from the hilt of his weapon, and he presses his lips together in what looks like defeat.

"I can hardly believe that."

"What?" I absently reply to the robin's gentle words as he twists me away, and we dance a few steps toward the middle. It's quite clear that he wants *all* of my attention. And he has it when I look up into his demanding eyes.

"That men haven't been fighting over your beauty every day in the past." He pulls me a little closer. The enticing smell of the wind clings to him and strokes my intrigue awake. It must come from the feathers on his mask. In this tight embrace, I can also feel how his body ripples with muscle under the orange shirt.

When my gaze trails down, he lets go of my hip and gently lifts my face with one knuckle under my chin. "From the moment you bumped into me, and your friends dragged you away, I wanted to learn more about you." His voice is as dark as his eyes, seductive and slow. As if he had trained to speak this way.

Mine, on the other hand, is squeaky as I grimace. "Sorry, I didn't mean to run you over."

He gives me a little push and twirls me under his arm. As soon as he holds me again, his gaze captures mine as if tethered by an invisible cord. "Don't be, sweet Riley. How else would I have met you tonight?"

A dreamy sigh threatens to escape me, but I keep it in check. I was absolutely right in my assumption that it always takes royalty for romance. Living proof holds me in his arms right now.

The song comes to an end, and while many couples leave the dance floor and others replace them, Jaccomo doesn't break our swaying. An insecure smile escapes me. "The song is over. Shouldn't we stop?"

"So that another *stranger* can abduct you?" Bringing his face very close to mine, he wrinkles his nose and slowly shakes his head. The gleam of desire in his eyes raises a nervous heat inside me as he whispers, "I don't think so."

When a new and slightly faster tune drifts from the string quartet, he picks up the pace, and we mingle with the dancers again. His determination makes me laugh. "But we can't dance the whole night."

A long moment of frowning passes as he considers that. Suddenly, something changes in his eyes—they blaze with delight. "You're right." He drops his hand from my side, but the other tightens around my fingers. Without warning, he cuts between the twirling couples and pulls me off the dance floor. "We should go outside. More privacy there." His sneer meets me over his shoulder. "And no one to steal you for another dance."

With this man, there really *is* no getting away. Giggling, I follow him off the dance floor and let him pull me toward the wide-open French doors. A refreshing waft of air hits me as we get closer, and a short stroll through the garden suddenly seems like a wonderful idea.

Hitching up my skirt with my free hand, I watch my steps and trust Jaccomo to lead us accident-free out of the ballroom. Only when he slows down, and I hear him say, "Phil… nice party!" do I lift my head.

We pass a group of seven. Ariel and Eric are the first ones I recognize, standing between Phillip and a man that I think is Prince Thomas. It should be him because he's holding Princess Rapunzel's hand, and she isn't hard to recognize. The mile-long golden braids wrapped into multiple coils and pinned to the back of her head are a dead giveaway.

The other two individuals with them are women I've never seen before. Their voile and wrap-around-style dress costumes in all shades of green and orange are a striking contrast to their flawless caramel skin. And standing between them, with the hand of the younger-looking exotic girl looped around his arm, is Prince Jacob.

"Casanova," Phillip acknowledges my escort with amusement in his voice. "Taking my runaway dance partner for a walk, I see."

Jaccomo laughs. "Too crowded in here."

I have the feeling I should apologize to Phillip for leaving him in the middle of our opening waltz. Only I can't bring myself to look at him as the fair prince with the silver mask holds every ounce of my attention captive. I don't even know how he's doing it because he doesn't speak a single word, nor does he move even one muscle. He just stands across from me, rigid and with his hands casually in his pockets as if he couldn't care less which beauty holds on to him.

I open my mouth to say something, to react in *some* way to the blue-eyed stare he freezes me with. But his silence is so loud, it overrides every thought in my mind. And then a firm tug on my hand makes me move. With my head turned over my shoulder, I find Jacob's gaze following us until the very moment we round the corner. A little shiver trails down my body.

I shake it off as Jaccomo guides me out onto the beautifully decorated patio. Light from the ballroom falls through the French doors and tints half of the paved area in warm shades of gold. The rest sleeps in warm shadows. A thick marble railing surrounds the semi-circular terrace, opening up to the side where a pebbled path leads away from the castle, deeper into the garden.

The few guests out here are mostly gathered close to the door. Jaccomo salutes them with a nod, and I tell them quietly, "Good evening." In the next second, I free my hand from his grip and run across the patio of the dreamy place. Lovely Chinese lanterns are strewn about the entire garden, glinting like fen fire in the dark. With my palms braced on the marble railing, I tilt back my head and close my eyes. A smile slips across my face. For one infinitesimal moment, it's only me in this amazing fairy tale. The crown is mine, the people in the ballroom are my guests, and the entire garden lies at my feet to explore if I want to.

I'm the princess of this castle.

A hand appears before me, holding a beautiful pink rose. "I hope you like flowers, my lady."

And my prince has just come to me…

Bewitched by the magic of the evening, I swirl around to Jaccomo and beam. "I love them."

But he doesn't give it to me. Instead, he breaks the stem, tosses it aside, and sticks the lovely blossom into my hair. "Just beautiful."

I lower my gaze. "Thank you, Lord Jaccomo."

"Will you wait here for me?" He strokes a wisp of hair behind my ear. "I'll run in and get us something to drink."

I nod. My first hour at the ball has been quite busy. I haven't had anything to drink since I came, and all the excitement has really dried me out.

For a moment, I gaze after him as he heads toward the

ballroom again, then I turn back to the banister and study the night sky above the garden. So many lights up there, so many stars to wish upon. And yet there's only one thing I really want for myself. To find true love tonight.

"They say all the stars up there are really the tears of the moon which he cried at every happy ending of a fairy tale in the world."

The soft caress of the voice behind me makes me close my eyes for a moment. "It is a lovely thought, isn't it?" I whisper. "Did the moon cry over your happy ending, too…"—I look over my shoulder—"…Jacob?"

He leans against a nearby apple tree, both hands in his pockets, and his sapphire eyes fixed on me, completely ignoring the glory of the stars above us.

"If he cries, they are tears of laughter, I'm afraid." With an almost sad chuckle, he casts a brief glance to the ground and then looks at me again. "Every story needs a villain. And they never win in the end."

Gripped by the sentiment of his words, I turn around and face him, clasping the edges of the marble banister behind my hips. "So you aren't a nice guy?"

Head tilted to one side, he thinks for a moment before he pushes away from the tree and ambles closer. Beside me, he stops and leans forward, bracing his forearms on the banister. "I'm still trying to figure that out," he says, his gaze wandering out to the garden.

Forehead creasing, I study him from the side. "How can you not know?"

"Sometimes, things aren't that easy, Riley."

I don't know what to say to that, but he has me more intrigued than ever. Jacob must sense my confusion because, after a moment, he straightens and turns around so we're both standing with our backs to the railing. A deep sigh leaves him as he glances down at me. "Let's take your new friend Casanova for instance. If I tell you that you'll be waiting in vain for the drink he probably offered to get you because he got...*distracted* inside, would that make me a good guy or a bad one?"

"What...?" The information takes a second to sink in. Then my entire body stiffens, and my gaze snaps past him to the French doors.

And there, by the sparkling pyramid of champagne glasses inside the ballroom, I find a striking orange shirt. Jaccomo holds a flute in his hand. A girl in green veils and a wrap-around dress in front of him does, too. Even from here, I can see how he cocks his head and smiles as he swipes a strand of her black hair behind her shoulder. And as he strokes her bare neck with his fingertips, he leans in and...

In that single moment, the ball loses all its magic for me. It just seeps out of my body like the color certainly seeps from my face. I swallow so hard, it hurts my throat, but it does little to give my voice more strength. "She was on your arm earlier." The words come out dry and flat.

Jacob glances at the couple near the champagne pyramid, clearly seeing what I do. "She was trying to get me to dance with her."

I sniff. "Why didn't you?"

His head turns my way, his fervent gaze burning the side of my face. "Because it's you I wanted to dance with."

Chapter 16

Like a stone gargoyle belonging to the castle, my fingers digging into the marble balustrade behind me where I stand out on the patio, I watch the scene unfold inside the ballroom. Jaccomo Casanova is not a gentleman. He's a heartbreaker.

"Riley?"

I feel a tender caress on my bare upper arm.

"It won't get easier if you continue watching this."

Jacob's soft voice finally rips me out of my stupor. My gaze skates across the place, frantically looking for an escape. Because going back inside is definitely not an option after seeing the prince who I thought might play a role in my new ever after kissing another girl. I swing around to Jacob. "You're right. It's just that I…" *Don't know where to go or what to do now.*

He searches my eyes for a moment. As if reading my thoughts, he offers me his elbow and a caring, soft smile along with it. "Would you like to take a walk through the garden?"

Walking sounds good. Garden sounds good. Away from this cursed stage of misery sounds awesome.

Straightening my spine and inhaling deeply, I slip my hand into the crook of his arm. When he starts walking, I hold him back, though. "Wait." I rip the rose out of my hair and bang it on the banister right where Jaccomo Casanova left me standing. "Okay, now we can go."

A tiny, pleased smirk appears on Jacob's face as he watches me a second longer before we finally stroll off.

Our steps crunch on the pebbled path leading away from the patio. The farther down we head into the garden, the more intense the lovely scent of the blooming trees and rosebushes grows. I find I can breathe again.

The ball was another failure in my prince hunt…so what? I went through a whole darn week of fails. This one won't kill me either. And for the little time I was a princess at Aurora and Phillip's ball, I really had fun.

"It's amazing, the multitude of emotions your face can shift through in less than two minutes."

When I turn my head toward Jacob, I notice that he's looking at me with a mix of wonder and amusement, and he's probably done that since we left the terrace.

Smirking right back, I drop a curtsy. "Glad I could entertain you, my lord."

"You never cease to, Riley." Now he laughs softly, but I throw him a confused look.

"You've only known me for an hour." Surely, I haven't entertained him with too many surprises in that short time, have I?

"Really?" He makes a funny, quirky face and presses the arm I'm holding tighter against his side, probably so I don't pull away as he kids me. "Felt like at least a week to me."

Ahead on the stone bridge over the Timeless Brook that takes a loop through Rory's garden, Hercules and Megara stroll toward us. No matter what kind of masks they wear, their Greek god outfits totally give them away. At the foot of the bridge, we nod in greeting, and they smile back at us, even if Meg looks like she has no idea who we are. Well, I can't speak for Prince Jacob, but I regularly drop into her gift shop of mythological things to chat with her.

Silence lingers between Jacob and me when we're alone again. We leave the brook behind, ambling on in the starlight. Soon, another type of sprinkling water sound drifts to us. Nearby is the duck pond with its ivory fountain in the middle. At the small junction, we take the path that runs down toward it. Lanterns still light the way this far out in the garden. Boy, once Rory gets started on something, she certainly doesn't do things by halves.

The dripping gets louder as we reach the pond surrounded by an old, belly-height stone wall. Resting my hands loosely on the ledge, I stop and watch the moonlight break like a heap of diamonds in the seven thin streams of water arching from the fountain spout.

Jacob stands beside me. He dips his finger into the pond and slowly stirs the water in small circles. I wonder what he's thinking about as he stares blankly into the swirl. Would he rather be somewhere else? Back in the ballroom with his friends perhaps?

With his mind elsewhere, I rub my upper arms because, suddenly, I feel alone, even though I'm standing right next to him. It only takes seconds before he looks up with a worried face, glancing at my arms then into my eyes. "Are you cold? Would you like my jacket?"

"No, thank you, I'm fine. It's a lovely night." It's nice to have him back from wherever he'd just gone, though. I drop my hands to grip my skirt instead of rubbing a non-existent chill from my skin. "But maybe we should go back. I don't want to keep you away from the feast for too long."

"Don't worry about that." Jacob gives me a sad smile that couldn't be more honest. "Actually, I didn't want to come to this ball at all."

Now that is a surprise. "Why not?"

"Mostly because of the company." He turns around

and hoists himself backward onto the wall ledge. Hands braced on the stone, he lets his feet dangle and looks at me sideways with a somewhat sheepish expression. "Crowded places make me nervous. Frankly, I'm not a big fan of royal show-offs."

With a curious tilt of my head, and my eyes narrowed on him, I walk backward a few steps to a projecting maple tree. My hands at my back as a buffer, I lean against the massive, knobby trunk. "Then why did you come?"

"I'm here because of a friend." He doesn't take his eyes off me, either, following my every move with his gaze. A shrug follows. "And of course, it's Phillip's birthday."

"Right. Your cousin." I almost forgot. "But the company clinging to your arm earlier didn't look too bad." Until she went for a drink with Jaccomo, of course.

His grimace makes me feel as if he read my last thought. "Scheherazade and her sister Sheila are just additional proof why I don't like princesses around me." He snorts. "They hang on to me. No doubt, some of them are really funny and nice. But mostly, there's something important missing from those girls, and they usually can't hold my attention for longer than five minutes."

I begin to nervously peel the bark from the trunk behind my bottom. "And what is that...something important?"

"I don't know." Briefly, he lowers his gaze to the path between us and then raises it back to my face. As he speaks again, his voice is lower than before. "A certain spark maybe."

We stare into each other's eyes for several quiet seconds. "If you detest princesses so much," I whisper eventually, "then why did you want to dance with me?"

Closing his eyes, he laughs softly. They gleam with amusement as he opens them again. "You aren't a princess, Riley."

I suck in a sharp breath between my teeth. "How can you say that?"

He takes his time to answer, putting me on edge. "Because you're different."

Okay, that could mean a thousand things. With wide eyes, I keep staring at him, my throat thickening too much to say anything yet. Jacob slides off the banister. With a slow prowl, he comes under the shelter of the overhanging branches speckled with a million reddish leaves. "Do you want to know what really made me walk up to you in the hallway?"

Pressing a little harder against the trunk, I raise my gaze the closer he draws until he's standing right in front of me with only a foot of space separating us. He braces his hand next to my head on the trunk and inches even closer. I can feel my heart knocking against the base of my throat.

"Any other girl in such a striking dress," he whispers, "wouldn't have waited a second to walk down the stairs. She would have been dying to show off to all the people in the hall." Gently, he places his other hand on my hip and really, I can't move, no matter how light his touch is. "But you hesitated. I saw how nervous you were. How you held on to the curtains for support. You looked intimidated by the thought of facing the ball."

Panic freezes me to the spot, and I swallow. What do I say now? Do I lie? Do I tell him the truth?

Do I kick his shin and run away without explanation?

His expression turns even softer. "Am I wrong?"

I inhale deeply, but my breath trembles as I slowly blink at him twice. "No, you're right. I'm not a princess." I sound as if a cheese grater has worked my throat. "I don't belong here. It was a stupid idea to come in the first place."

Jacob doesn't seem to judge me, he only appears curious and…caring. "Where *do* you belong?"

It's hard to hold his insistent gaze. Impossible. I break out of his spell, sidestep him, and take a few quick strides down the path. Then I stop and whirl around. "In the woods. It's the only place I've ever known as home."

There has never been a time in my life when I longed for my red cloak more than in this moment. If Jacob heads off now, knowing the truth, and leaves me behind just like Jaccomo did earlier, I could hide in it and wouldn't feel so lost again.

But the prince doesn't run away. On the contrary, he walks toward me, but for every step he takes closer, I take one away. I stumble backward until he smiles, and I realize how stupid I must look. My feet grow roots, and I finally let him come closer.

Jacob takes both of my hands in his and tugs me over

to the duck pond where he leans against the wall again. "You seem like you have an interesting story to tell." He doesn't free my hands but keeps me there right before him, almost between his spread legs. Underneath that silver mask, the marvelous night sky reflects off his gorgeous eyes. He blinks and gives me the softest of smiles. "What's your tale, Riley?"

His genuine interest coaxes a sigh from me, and I lower my lashes. "There's not much to tell, really. I just spend a lot of time in the forest."

"What do you do there?"

I shrug. "Talk to someone and try to save my family from an attack."

Jacob reaches out and, with a finger under my chin, he lifts my gaze back to his warm eyes. "Do you get a happy ending?"

"I do…but not the way I wish."

His curiosity is obviously growing as he cocks his head. "What way would that be?"

Maybe it's a bad idea to tell him this. But since he already figured out that I'm not a princess, I can probably tell him everything now. Also, it strangely feels as if I can be honest with him, and he won't laugh. After a long moment with my lips pressed into a hard line, the quiet words finally slip out. "I never get kissed."

His hand still rests lightly against my neck, but now his thumb skims gently along my jaw. His fingers are warm and tender, his touch amazingly pleasant. "What a shame…and a waste." The next moment, his hand drops as if he just realized that he'd gone too far. Bracing himself on the stone barrier with his hands on either side of his hips, he frowns and clears his throat. "Isn't there a guy in your story?"

At the memory of my time with Jack this past week, my heart glows unexpectedly, and my grin widens. "Oh, sure there is." Even if he's a Wolf most of the time.

Jacob narrows his eyes. A cynical snort escapes him. "So he's an idiot?"

His joke makes me snicker. "No. Jack isn't an idiot. He's smart and funny." My thoughts drift off to the night when he locked himself in Phillip's dungeon to keep me safe from the beast. "And caring…" I add in a strangely hoarse voice. And suddenly, I really miss him. "In fact, he's one of the best men I know."

"Sounds as if you like this guy a lot," he taunts, throwing me yet another sideways glance and a lopsided grin. "Do I have a rival?"

"A rival?" A surprised laugh escapes me as I back away. "Why, Jacob? Are you fighting for my heart?"

He pushes himself off the stone wall. Slowly, like a wolf on the prowl, he comes forward, licking his lips. His blue eyes take on a darker gleam in the night with each step he takes toward me. I didn't realize I was drawing away until the knobby trunk of the maple tree is suddenly at my back again, stopping my escape.

With my mouth slightly parted, I completely forget to

breathe as he shapes his palms to my cheeks. We look into each other's eyes for an endless moment. I think my heart disappeared because I can't feel it beating anymore. Tilting his head down a little, Jacob strokes his thumb across my bottom lip. His gaze drops to my mouth and then moves back to my eyes. One second later, his lashes lower, and my eyes fall shut, too.

"Fighting for your heart, I am. Didn't you notice that yet?" he whispers.

And then he catches my upper lip in a tender, sweet kiss. My mouth shapes against his out of instinct. It only lasts for two seconds, but a thousand little pinpricks of pleasure race through me at the touch. His lips leave mine, only to come right back for another soft caress and this time, he puts a little more pressure in the embrace. The third time he does it, my mouth opens, and his tongue delves in. It sweeps against my own, once, slowly. Then he ends our kiss the same way it began, with a gentle catch of my upper lip.

For the past half-minute, I've been melting between him and the tree. Everything around me feels like a bed of cozy clouds. I want to stay in this dreamy moment forever and never wake again. But when his lips detach and I can only feel his warm breath on my skin, my eyes flutter open.

Sparkling sapphires linger before me.

Still in a daze, I blink up at him. So this is what I've been missing out on all these years. My princess friends get kissed every day—inside their stories and out. They found people to give their hearts to from the moment their tales began.

For me, it took forever.

Jacob's eyes soften behind the silver mask as he smiles. He brushes his hands down my gloved arms and then laces our fingers together, keeping us close. Blissfully smiling back at him, I draw in a deep breath.

A single, light breeze wafts around us, stirring the skirt of my dress. My skin rises in goosebumps and, all of a sudden, there's a shift. I can't even say if it's just inside my body or around us, but it feels as if something...cracked. Like a rift in polar ice.

The sensation is gone as fast as it appeared, taking the tingle from my skin with it. I wonder if Jacob felt it, too. He has become very still. His gaze hasn't left mine in the past three seconds, but his hands tightened around mine in an almost worrisome way.

When I try to flex my fingers, he releases me immediately, obviously realizing what he's doing. And that it hurt. Narrowing his eyes, he quickly shakes his head and clears his throat. Apparently, it wasn't just me who felt...whatever that was.

I open my mouth to ask him about it, but the words never come. My eyes shoot up, and I stiffen. Behind his shoulder, right there on the duck pond, the Fairy Godmother appears. She levitates a few inches above the water, tapping her index finger on her left wrist.

The time? Yeah, yeah... I promised not to crash at

Rory's castle, and I won't. But the night has only just begun, and it has turned into something so beautiful. She can't expect me to go home right now. If she's tired, no one's asking her to stay.

Jacob studies my face for a split second. Then he turns around, his forehead creasing in suspicion, but the fairy popped out and vanished seconds before he saw her. When he turns his head back to me, the furrows on his brows deepen. "Is everything okay?"

Shutting off my short irritation, I smile at him, which actually feels more like a cramping grimace. "Yes, everything's perfect."

Except the fairy lady has just reappeared between the bushes, frantically waving her arms as if she's mad.

I sling my hand through Jacob's arm and pull him away from the tree, casting him a pleading look. "Can we walk a bit?"

He hesitates a second, but then he bends his arm and tucks the other hand into his pocket. "Sure…"

I throw a glance over my shoulder, morosely narrowing my gaze at the brash woman. It can't hurt to just stay another hour or two, right? Dawn is far away, and I swear I'll be lying in my bed before the sun creeps over the horizon.

We stroll toward the wide stone bridge across the Timeless Brook that we crossed to get here. The reverse flow of the water has a soothing effect on me. I dare another short look behind us and exhale in relief when I see that the Fairy Godmother is gone.

Jacob's puzzled eyes try to find mine when I turn forward again, but I'm quick to escape his gaze. He doesn't need to know that a crazy, tired chaperone is weaseling around.

"Riley, did I do something wrong?"

My gaze is fastened on the ground, my steps slowing to match his reluctant pace. "No. No, you didn't. That was...what you did..." I look at him, and a deep sigh leaves me, bringing back all the dreamy feelings of earlier when we kissed. "It was beautiful."

"Then why are you being so evasive now?"

"I'm not. I just..." *Freeze.*

My expression derails as the fairy lady appears again behind him, hovering over the little river. This time, she brought a grandfather clock and pushes it down onto the water as if the surface is made of concrete—which maybe it is because, after a quick splash, the clock keeps standing there. What is her darn problem? Is it her mission now to ruin my perfect night with the Prince from the Snow Plains?

"You...what?" Jacob prompts me with a worried frown.

"Nothing." Tense and angry, I stride faster, trying hard to ignore the fairy on the water. "We should go back to the feast." Hopefully, the crowd will keep her away.

His hand snatches my wrist, and he hauls me back. "Stop!"

I gasp as I nearly bump into his chest.

"What's wrong?" he demands, the lines around his mouth hardening.

I remain silent because I really don't know what to say when the Fairy Godmother is acting like a maniac behind him, floundering and pedaling in the air. She doggedly slaps her wand against the glass of the clock face. Behind it, the minute hand just begins to bridge the last minute to midnight.

Wait! Midnight? There was something happening at midnight, right? What was it? *What was it?!*

The fairy grabs a fistful of her skirt, shaking it. Oh crap, my gown!

FIRST STRIKE OF THE CLOCK.
My mouth drops open. *Ugh!*

SECOND STRIKE OF THE CLOCK.
"If the kiss was a mistake, then tell me." Jacob doesn't let go of my hand, but the silver-framed sapphires turn soft as they plead with me. "Don't just run away."

THIRD STRIKE OF THE CLOCK.
Dang, I might have no other choice!

FOURTH STRIKE OF THE CLOCK.
"I'm so sorry, but it's late. I need to leave!" Really, *really* fast!

FIFTH STRIKE OF THE CLOCK.

My hand is caught. I can't get away, and my heart starts to flutter against my throat like a lunatic canary in a cage. "Please, Prince Jacob, you must let me go. I can't stay here."

SIXTH STRIKE OF THE CLOCK.

"Only for a few more minutes, I beg you."

SEVENTH STRIKE OF THE CLOCK.

Not even for a few more seconds.

I tug harder at my hand, whining in panic as I do a funky version of the potty dance.

EIGHTH STRIKE OF THE CLOCK.

My wailing stirs his mercy, and he finally lets me go. But his torn look breaks my heart. I hitch up my skirt, ready to run. "I don't want to go. Really. I wish I could stay the entire night out here in the garden with you, but I can't."

NINTH STRIKE OF THE CLOCK.

I dash off the bridge.

"I need to tell you something. It's important," his desperate voice follows me.

TENTH STRIKE OF THE CLOCK.

I swirl around and run back, but not because of his

pleading. I just realized I was heading deeper into the garden. With my dress disappearing in two more seconds, I should probably head for the exit instead.

ELEVENTH STRIKE OF THE CLOCK.

Trembling in terror, I skitter to a stop in front of Jacob once more. His expression is hopeful now. I grimace. Holy broken glass slipper, he can't see me pop into my underwear. It will be the death of me. There must be another way out.

Oh, wait! Did I say slipper? Heck, the shoes I'm wearing are from Kansas!

TWELFTH STRIKE OF THE CLOCK.

I click my heels together.

To be continued...

Lose yourself in the fairy tale sequel!

ANNA KATMORE
A Wolf
IN HER WAY

WHISPERING PAGES, book 2

When Red Riding Hood learned that love doesn't need a crown.

I've been gone from the woods for only two days, and suddenly everyone is thrilled to see me again. Even Jack. Especially Jack.

He kisses me like he's afraid I might disappear if he lets go—but the timing couldn't be worse. What is he thinking? That one hard kiss can stop me from finding my prince from the ball?
Jack says I wouldn't recognize love if it ran me down with a coach. Please. I should teach him a thing or two about love.

I'm going on this journey! He can come with me… or not.

Jack here. And for the record? Following her was a terrible idea.
The farther we travel, the worse this gets—winter nights, bad plans, and the crushing realization that asking Phillip for help with the whole prince situation was a huge mistake. I'm in deep, ugly trouble.

All I wanted was to prove I'm enough without a crown.
So why does everything feel like it's falling apart?

Can't we just start over?
Please?

More books by Anna Katmore

ON THIN ICE
Counting Fireflies
Splintered North
*

Seventeen Butterflies

GROVER BEACH PLAYERS
Play With Me
Ryan Hunter
T Is For…
Dating Trouble
The Trouble with Dating Sue
The Impossible Bet
Taming Chloe Summers

CRUSHED HEARTS
Unfair Love
Broken Dawn
Awaking Trust

DREAMS OF NEVER EVER
Neverland
Pan's Revenge

WHISPERING PAGES
No Prince for Riding Hood
A Wolf in her Way

*

Eloyn
My Secret Vampire
You were my Fairy Tale

About the author

"I write stories because I can't breathe without."

Anna Katmore lives in an enchanting world of her own. It's a place where logic waits patiently at the gate and only dreamers are allowed to enter. Beware, though, once you step through, you may never wish to leave again.

Disney isn't just her passion; it's her attitude toward life. If she could, she'd wrap the world in a little stardust and save it from itself. Her patronus is a wolf. Her wand is a broken twig from an apple tree, 13¾ inches long, yet full of charm. And although there's always glitter on her shoes, she keeps a safe distance from Cinderella's glass slippers. Too risky, something might break.

For more magic, visit www.annakatmore.com